I0536384

THE RADIO DETECTIVES

THE RADIO DETECTIVES

A. HYATT VERRILL

AN A HYATT VERRILL BOOK

AN A HYATT VERRILL BOOK

Published by Wildside Press, LLC
www.wildsidebooks.com

CHAPTER I

TOM TAKES UP A RADIO

"Oh, Dad! I've made a new set," cried Tom, as he entered the dining room.

"That so, Son?" replied Mr. Pauling interestedly. "Seems to me you boys do nothing but junk your sets as fast as you make them and build others. Does this one work better than the last?"

"It's a peach!" declared Tom enthusiastically. "Just wait till you see it and listen to the music coming in."

"I'll come up after dinner," his father assured him. "Let me know when the fun begins. I've some papers to go over in the library first."

Throughout the meal the talk was all of radio, in which Tom and his boy friends had become madly interested and in which Tom's father and mother had encouraged him.

"Go to it, Tom," his father had said when the boy had glowingly expatiated on the wonderful things he had heard on a friend's instrument and had asked his father's permission to get a set. "I'm glad you're interested in it," he had continued. "It's going to be a big thing in the future and the more you learn about it the better. But begin at the beginning, Tom. Don't be satisfied merely with buying instruments and using them. Learn the whole thing from the bottom up and use your mechanical ability to build instruments and to make improvements. Wish they'd had something as fascinating when I was a kid."

Tom had lost no time in availing himself of his father's permission, and of the roll of bills which had accompanied it, and there was no prouder or more excited boy in Greater New York than Tom Pauling when he triumphantly brought home his little crystal receiving set and exhibited it to his parents.

"I can't understand how a little box with a few nickel-plated screws and some knobs can do all the things you say," was his mother's comment. "But then," she added, "I never could understand anything mechanical or electrical. Even a phonograph or an electric light is all a mystery to me."

Mr. Pauling looked the instrument over carefully and listened attentively to Tom's graphic explanation of detectors, tuners, condensers, etc.

"H-m-m," he remarked, "I guess I'll have to take a back seat now, Son. You evidently have a pretty good grip on the fundamentals. Sorry I can't help you any, but it's all Greek to me, I admit."

"Oh, it's all mighty simple," Tom assured him. "Frank's coming over this afternoon and we're going to put up the aërial and then you and mother can hear the music and songs from Newark to-night."

But despite the fact that Mrs. Pauling declared it the most remarkable thing she had ever seen or heard, and his father complimented him, Tom was far from satisfied with his first set. He didn't like the idea of being obliged to sit with head phones clamped to his ears in order to hear the music from the big broadcasting stations; he felt that it was mighty unsatisfactory for only one person to hear the sounds at one time and he soon found that despite every effort he was continually interrupted by calls and messages from near-by amateur stations.

Being of a naturally inventive and mechanical mind and remembering his father's advice to try to improve matters, he spent all his spare time studying the radio magazines, haunting the stores where radio supplies and instruments were sold and arguing about and discussing various devices and sets with his boy friends. Hardly a day passed that he did not arrive at his home carrying some mysterious package or bundle. Accompanied by his chum Frank, from the time school was over until late in the evening he kept himself secluded in his den while faint sounds of hammering or of animated conversation might have been heard within.

"What's all the mystery, Son?" his father had asked on one occasion. "Going to spring some big invention on an unsuspecting world?"

Tom laughed. "Not quite, Dad," he replied, "but I'm going to give you and mother a surprise pretty soon."

When at last all was ready and his parents were invited to Tom's holy of holies they were indeed surprised. Upon a small table were various instruments and devices and a seeming tangle of wires, while, tucked away on a bookshelf, was the little crystal set which had so recently been Tom's pride and joy.

And still greater was their surprise when, after busying himself over the instruments, the faint sounds of music filled the room, coming mysteriously from the apparent odds and ends upon the table.

"It's all homemade," Tom had explained proudly. "But it works. Frank and I rigged it up just as an experiment. Now I'm going to reassemble it and put it in a case and have a regular set."

"Wait a minute, Tom," his father had interrupted. "You'll have to explain a bit. If that lot of stuff can give so much better results than the set you bought, why didn't you make it in the first place, and what's the difference anyway?"

"Well, you see, Dad," Tom tried to explain, "I had to start at the bottom as you said and a crystal set's the bottom. This is a vacuum tube set. Those things like little electric lights are the tubes and they're the heart of the whole thing, and I've a one-step amplifier and that has to have another tube. I didn't have enough pocket money to buy everything so Frank lent me some of his. You see it's this way—"

"Never mind about the technicalities," laughed his father. "As I said before, go to it. Get what you need and keep busy. It's a fine thing for you boys. Now turn her on again, or whatever you call it, and let's hear some more music."

From that time, Tom's progress was rapid although, as his

father had jokingly remarked, the boy's chief occupation appeared to be building sets one day only to tear them down and reconstruct them the next.

Tom's room had assumed the appearance of an electrical supply shop. Tools, wire, sheet brass, bakelite, hard rubber knobs, odds and ends of metal, coils and countless other things had taken the places of books, skates, baseball bats and papers, and the fiction magazines had given way to radio periodicals, blue prints and diagrams. Mrs. Pauling was in despair and complained to her husband that Tom was making a dreadful mess of his room and expressed fears that he might get hurt fooling with electricity.

"Don't you fret over that," her husband had advised. "Tom and his friends are having the time of their lives. As long as they are learning something of value, what does it matter if they do keep his room in a mess? Besides, it's clean dirt you know—and it's orderly disorder if you know what I mean. They're exploring a new world and haven't time to look after such trifles as having a place for everything and everything in its place. That will come later. Just now they are fired with the zeal and enthusiasm of great inventors and scientists. We mustn't interfere with them—such feelings come to human beings but once in a lifetime. I consider this radio craze the best thing for boys that ever occurred. It gives them an interest, it's educational, it keeps them off the street and occupies their brains and hands at the same time. Do you know, if I didn't have my time so fully occupied, I believe I'd get bitten by the bug myself. Besides, they may really discover something worth while. I was talking to Henderson of our staff to-day—he had charge of our radio work during the war—and he tells me some of the best inventions in radio have been made by amateurs—quite by accident too. I expect Tom knows that and that's what makes the kids so keen on the subject—it's a wonderful thought to feel you may stumble on some little thing that will revolutionize a great science at any moment."

"Yes, I suppose you're right, Fred," agreed Tom's mother resignedly. "But I do wish it were possible to have boys amuse themselves without tracking shavings all over the halls and burning holes in their clothes and having grimy fingers."

But Tom's mother need not have worried. Gradually order came out of chaos. As the boys progressed, they found that the accumulation of odds and ends and the disorder interfered with their work; many experimental instruments and devices had been discarded and were now tossed into a junk box in the closet; a neat work table with the tools handily arranged had been rigged up and Tom and Frank had developed a well-equipped and orderly little workshop with the completed instruments on an improvised bench under the window.

Both Mr. and Mrs. Pauling had noticed the gradual improvement, as from time to time they had been summoned by Tom to witness demonstrations of the latest products of the boys' brains and hands, and both parents congratulated the boys on their handiwork and the strides they had made. So, on the night when Tom had assured his father that his latest set was a "peacherino," the two grownups entered a room which, as Mr. Pauling expressed it, reminded him of a wireless on a ship.

And then, after Tom with the glowing eyes and flushed face of an inventor and the pride of a showman, had exhibited his latest achievement and had explained its mysteries in terms which were utterly unintelligible to his parents, they sat spellbound as the strains of a military band fairly filled the room.

"Fine!" declared Mr. Pauling when the concert ended. "You have got a 'peacherino' as you call it."

"Oh, that's nothing," declared Tom deprecatingly. "I can get Pittsburgh and I can get spark messages from Cuba and Canada, and last night I picked up a message from Balboa. I'll hear England and France before I'm satisfied."

"Bully!" exclaimed his father. "Tell you what I'll do. I'm off to Cuba and the Bahamas, Monday, you know. I'll radio from the ship on the way down and after I get there you can see if you can pick up my messages direct and can talk back."

"Oh, I can't do that, yet," declared Tom. "I haven't a sending set. You have to get a license for that, but I'm going to get at it right away. It will be fine to be able to hear you. I'll bet I can get your messages from Cuba and Nassau. Say, it will be almost like hearing you talk."

"How shall I address them?" chuckled his father. "Tom Pauling, The Air?"

"Gee! I hadn't thought of that," ejaculated Tom. "I haven't any call letters—only sending stations have them—I've got it! When you send a message, just address it as if it were a regular message and then I'll know it's for me. And send them the same time every time—then I'll be sure to be here and waiting to get them."

"Righto," agreed his father. "I'll be sending a good many official messages, I expect, and I can get them all off together each day—say 7:45. How will that be?"

"That'll be fine," assented Tom. "I'll be here at half-past seven every night listening. Say, Dad, do you suppose those smuggler fellows use radio?"

"Why, I don't know; what made you ask?"

"Oh, I just happened to think of it," replied Tom. "I guess your speaking of sending official messages and starting for Cuba and the Bahamas just put it in my head."

"Well, if we don't find how they're getting liquor into the States by wholesale pretty quick, I'll begin to think they're sending the booze in by radio," laughed Mr. Pauling. "It's the most mysterious thing we've been up against yet. Can't get a clue. Perhaps they are using radio to warn one another, or maybe they're onto our codes. Suppose you keep track of any odd messages you hear, Tom. I don't suppose there's anything in it, but it will give you another interest and one never knows what may happen through chance or accident. Remember that coup I told you about that we made during the war—that meaningless message that passed all the censors and that, by pure accident, led to the capture of the worst lot of German plotters in the country?"

But Frank had not heard the story and so, from radio, the conversation drifted to Mr. Pauling's experiences as an officer of the Department of Justice during the war and from that to his present problem of tracing to its source the mysterious influx of liquor which was flooding New York and other ports despite every effort of the government to stop it.

It was on this work that he was leaving for the West Indies, and long after he and Mrs. Pauling had left the room, Tom and Frank remained, talking earnestly, and with boyish imagination discussing the possibilities of aiding the government through picking up some stray information from the air by means of their instruments.

"We ought to have better sets," declared Tom. "These are all right for getting the broadcasted entertainments and spark signals, but we can't get the long waves from the big stations. And we don't always get farther than Arlington or Pittsburgh with this. Last night, we heard Balboa, but the night before that we couldn't get Havana. If we're going to hear Dad from Nassau or Cuba we want a set we can depend upon."

"I'll tell you what we'll do," replied Frank. "Let's put everything that we both have together and have a fine set here in your room. I'll bring my stuff down and we can work together—have duplicate sets and everything—and I'll just keep that little old set of mine so I can use it when I happen to be home."

"That's a good idea," agreed Tom, "Dad's so interested in our work I can spend a lot more money on instruments and he won't mind and school will soon be over and we can devote all our time to it. Gosh, I bet we have the best sets of any boys in the whole of New York! Say, won't it be great when we can hear messages from England and Germany and France?"

"Yes, and we want to get busy on a sending set too. It's twice as much fun when we can talk to others as well as hear them. And say! my folks are going to Europe next month. If your mother and father don't mind I could stay here with you."

"That's bully! Of course mother won't mind and Dad will be glad to have you," declared Tom. "We're not going any place this summer and so we can give all our vacation to radio. Say, we may make some big discovery or invention. I was reading the other day about how many things there are to be done in radio yet and the fellow that wrote it said he believed some of the big things would be discovered by boys or beginners accidentally."

Mrs. Pauling was very glad to have Frank plan to stay with Tom while his parents were absent and for several days the two boys were busy packing up Frank's radio outfits and carrying them to Tom's house.

When at last everything was there the boys had a veritable treasure trove of materials, for Frank had not been stinted in the amount he could spend on good tools, supplies and instruments and, while he did not possess the mechanical or inventive ability of Tom, yet he was a very careful and painstaking worker and everything he had was of the best.

Tom, on the other hand, preferred to make everything himself and, although his father was willing to let him have any sum within reason to carry on his radio work, he spent most of the money for tools and supplies and had built a number of special instruments which even Frank admitted were big improvements over ready-made devices. In addition, he had a very complete library of radio books as well as scrapbooks filled with clippings from the radio columns of the various newspapers and periodicals. Hence the two boys made most excellent partners for carrying on their experiments and building their sets. Fortunately, too, they were not the type of boys who soon become tired of a subject and take up one fad after another and, while they were both strong, red-blooded, out-of-door boys, always ready for the most strenuous games, long hikes or hunting and fishing, they found radio so much more fascinating than football, baseball or other sports that practically everything else had been abandoned.

CHAPTER II—MYSTERIOUS MESSAGES

For the next few days the boys were very busy perfecting their instruments and, when Mr. Pauling bade Tom and his mother good-by and sailed southward, Tom assured him that he would be able to pick up any messages he sent.

"Maybe I'll surprise you by sending a message," he declared. "I'm going to apply for a license next week and make a sending set. Of course it won't be able to send clear to Cuba or Nassau, but freak messages *do* go long distances sometimes and anyway, I can get in touch with your ship before you reach port coming back."

"Great!" exclaimed his father heartily. "And don't forget about stray messages—you may help us out yet. I spoke to Henderson about your idea that the bootleggers were using radio and he says he should not be a bit surprised. They're right up to date in their methods, you know."

That evening, Tom and Frank hurried to their sets promptly at 7:30 accompanied by Mrs. Pauling who seemed as interested as the boys in the result of their first attempt to pick up a message intended for them. She was rather disappointed, however, when Tom clamped on his phones and told her she wouldn't be able to hear anything.

"You see," he explained, "if the message comes in, it will be just code signal—dots and dashes in International Morse—and wouldn't mean anything to you and I might miss it if I used the loud speaker."

Slowly the minutes slipped by. From out of the silent air came various sounds to the boys' impatient ears—little buzzing dots and dashes from local stations; the faint sounds of a phonograph from some amateur's radiophone; fragments of speech from a broadcasting station. Carefully the two waiting, expectant boys tuned their instruments, for they had taken the precaution of asking the wireless operator on the ship what wave length he used and with their sets tuned as nearly to this as possible they cut out the amateur senders with their short wave lengths and the broadcasting stations with their evening entertainments on 360 meter waves and heard only the meaningless or uninteresting Morse messages passing from ships to shore or vice versa.

Over and over Tom and Frank glanced anxiously at the little nickel-plated clock ticking merrily on its shelf, until at last the hands pointed to 7:45 and the boys fairly thrilled with excitement. Would they hear the message from the speeding ship? Would they pick up that one message that they were expecting? Would they, in a moment more, be listening to the dots and dashes that represented Mr. Pauling's words? Neither boy was yet expert at reading Morse if sent rapidly, but the wireless man aboard the *Havana* had laughingly agreed to send Mr. Pauling's messages slowly and the boys were not worried on that score.

Suddenly, to Tom's ears, came a sharp buzz—faint and blurred, and with trembling fingers he tuned his set, adjusted the variable condenser and as the short, staccato sounds grew sharp, loud and clear he knew that the long-hoped-for message was coming to his ears. "Dah, dah dah dah, dah dah, dee dah dah dee, dee dah, dee dee dah, dee dah dee dee, dee dee, dah dee, dah dah dee," came the dots and dashes, sent slowly as if by an amateur and mentally Tom translated them. Yes, there was no doubt of it, TOM PAULING were the words the dots and dashes spelled and Tom's heart beat a trifle faster and his face flushed with excitement as he heard his own name coming out of space and realized that, across a hundred miles and more of tossing sea, his father was talking to him and steadily he jotted down the letters as they buzzed in dots and dashes through the air from the distant ship.

"Hurrah!" he fairly yelled, as with the final "dee dah dee dah dee" the operator signified that the message was finished. "Hurrah! I got it. See, here 'tis, Mother!"

Frank also had received the message on his set and the two compared the letters they had written down.

"Of course we made some mistakes," explained Tom as his mother puzzled over the unpunctuated, apparently meaningless letters. "See," he continued, "you have to separate the letters into words and sentences and this one should be an "N" instead of an "A" and I guess this is a "D" instead of a "B," Frank's got it that way. One's a dash and three dots and the other's a dash and two dots."

As he spoke, Tom was busily copying the letters and forming words and presently showed his mother the finished message. "That's it," he announced proudly. "Just think of Dad talking to us—and he'll do it every night all the way down and after he gets there. Gosh! It's funny to think we can hear from him that way. Say, isn't radio great?"

"But I thought you could hear him talking," said his mother in rather disappointed tones. "He could send messages that way by the regular radio companies or by cable."

"Of course he could," agreed Tom somewhat disturbed because his mother was not more enthusiastic over his achievement. "But you see the fun is in getting it ourselves this way. It wouldn't be any sport to have the messages brought in an envelope like ordinary telegrams. Gee! I just wish we could hear him talk over the phones. Some of the ships have talked with the shore farther away than he is, but I guess the *Havana's* radio isn't up-to-date."

"I think it's fine and splendid of you boys to be able to do this," declared his mother. "What I meant was, that I had expected to hear your father's voice and I really *was* disappointed when I found it was so different."

"Well, I'm going to fix a set to talk back to him," said Tom. "And just as soon as I get the sending set done we'll get to work and make a better receiving set, won't we, Frank?"

"You bet!" agreed Frank. "Perhaps by the time your father is on the way back we can really talk to him."

"Now let's have some music," suggested Tom, and for the next hour they all listened to the broadcasting station's program as the loud speaker filled the room with the sounds of music, singing, speeches and news.

For the next three nights the two boys picked up Mr. Pauling's messages regularly and were as proud as peacocks when they managed to get the first message from Havana telling of his safe arrival in Cuba. And by their enthusiastic studies and the practice they gained by deciphering the messages, the boys were successful in passing the required examination and proudly exhibited their license to maintain and operate a sending station.

It was a red letter day in their lives when they at last had the transmitting set in working order and flashed a message into the night, to have it promptly answered by an unknown boy in Garden City. Each night, too, they sent out messages directed to their father in the vain hope that, by some chance or by the same mysterious combination of conditions which had wafted other messages to vast distances beyond the range of the instruments, their words might be picked up in Havana or Nassau; but no reply came and at last they gave up in despair.

Then, their sending set being no longer a novelty, the boys set diligently to work on other matters and worked early and late.

"What on earth is that?" asked Tom's mother, when finally the new idea had assumed concrete form and she was invited to witness a demonstration. "It looks like some sort of a huge birdcage," she continued as she seated herself and glanced at the wooden framework wound with wire that stood on a small table.

"Well, I don't suppose you can understand," replied Tom, with the superior air of one who is master of an art beyond ordinary comprehension, "but I'll try to explain. That's a loop aërial."

"But I thought the aërial was that wire clothesline-like affair on the roof," objected Mrs. Pauling. "You see," she laughed, "I *am* beginning to learn a little."

Tom grinned, "Oh, yes, that's an aërial, too," he replied. "But this is another kind. With this we don't need any ground or lead-ins or lightning switches. And it's directional too. That is," he hastened to explain, "by turning it one way or another we can pick up signals from certain directions and not from others. Some people call them compass aërials and they're used on ships for locating other vessels or for finding their way. And besides, they cut out a lot of static."

"Now please, Tom, what *is* all this you're talking about? What *is* static?"

"Well that's mighty hard to explain," said Tom, scratching his head reflectively. "It's a sort of electricity in the air—lots of it around when there are thunderstorms and lightning."

"Lightning!" exclaimed his mother. "Do be careful, fooling with all these things, Tom. I'm always afraid you'll get a fearful shock or something."

"Nonsense," laughed Tom. "Static doesn't hurt any one and lightning won't do any harm. An aërial is just like a lightning-rod and if it's struck the lightning is just carried down to the ground harmlessly; but this loop aërial's different. Now let's hear how it works."

Adjusting the instruments and attaching the loud-speaker, Tom slowly turned the cagelike affair about and suddenly, as it faced the west, the sounds of music burst out from the horn.

"There 'tis!" cried Tom, exultantly. "That's Newark. Now, see here." As he spoke, he swung the loop aërial to one side, and instantly, the music died out. "Now, listen carefully," he continued and turned the loop slowly around until, somewhat fainter, the sounds of a human voice came from the loud-speaker. "That's Pittsburgh," declared Tom. "Now you see how it works. If it's turned towards Newark we get Newark and if towards Pittsburgh we get that."

"Yes, it's all very interesting," admitted his mother. "But what advantage is it? You used to hear both Newark and Pittsburgh with the aërial on the roof."

"Oh, it's no advantage for ordinary work," replied Tom. "But it's a fine thing in some ways. Now, for instance, if we heard a fellow's message and didn't know where it came from we could tell by turning this back and forth until we got his direction. Then, if we wanted to locate him exactly, we could put it up somewhere else and in that way we could find out just where he was. Frank and I have a particular scheme in hand, but that's a secret and I'm not ready to tell it yet."

His mother laughed. "I'm not a bit curious," she declared. "I suppose some day I'll wake up to find you two boys have astonished the world."

But had Frank and Tom told Mrs. Pauling what their secret was she would have been both curious and surprised. Several times within the preceding weeks the boys, listening at their instruments, had received messages which they could not locate. At first they had given no heed to these, thinking they were merely from some amateur, but when, after repeated requests for the unknown's call letters, no answer was received and the messages abruptly ceased, the two boys began to be curious.

"There's something mighty funny about him," declared Frank. "Every time we answer him or ask a question he shuts up like a clam. Say, Tom, maybe he's a crook or a bootlegger."

"More likely some amateur sending without a license and afraid the government inspector will get after him," suggested Tom. "But I *would* like to find out who it is."

A few days later Frank, who was poring over the latest issue of a radio magazine, uttered an exclamation. "Gosh! here's the scheme," he cried. "Now we can find out who that mysterious chap is."

"What's the big idea?" queried Tom, who was busy making a new vario-coupler.

"Loop aërial," replied his chum. "Here's an article all about it. It says they're used aboard ships to find the location of other vessels and are called compass aërials."

Tom dropped his work and hurried to Frank's side.

"Well," he remarked, after a few moments' study of the article and the diagrams, "I don't see how that would work in our case. It says one ship can find another or can work its way into port by using the loop aërial like a compass, but the trouble is the ship's moving and so the thing will work, but we can't go running around New York City or the state with a set in one hand and a big loop aërial in the other."

"No," admitted Frank rather regretfully, "but we can tell in which direction his station is."

"Yes, and it will be fun to make one and experiment with it," agreed Tom, "especially as the article says the thing cuts out static and interferences and it's getting on towards warm weather now when the air will be full of static."

"Well, let's make one then," suggested Frank.

As a result, the boys had constructed their loop aërial and a special set to go with it and the very first time they tested the odd affair they were overjoyed at the result. Again they had picked up the messages which had aroused their curiosity and, by turning the loop one way and then another, they were soon convinced that the sender had a station to the southeast of their own.

"Well, that's settled," announced Tom, "and the only things southeast of here are the East Side, the river and Brooklyn. That fellow is not far away—he's using a very short wave and his messages are strong. I'll bet he's right here in New York."

"I guess you're right," agreed Frank, "but that doesn't do much good. There's an awful lot of the city southeast from here."

"Sure there is," said Tom, "but, after all, what do we care. I still think he's just some unlicensed chap—probably some kid over on the East Side who can't pass an examination or get a license and is just having a little fun on the quiet."

This conversation took place two days before Tom received his father's message telling of his safe arrival in Cuba and no more messages from the mysterious stranger were heard until the day after Mr. Pauling's message had been received.

Then, as Tom was listening at the loop aërial set and idly turned the aërial about, he again picked up the well-known short-wave messages. Heretofore the messages had been meaningless sentences in code, dots and dashes which the boys out of curiosity had jotted down only to find them devoid of any interest—items regarding shipping which Tom had declared had been culled from the daily shipping lists and were being sent merely for practice—and so now, from mere habit, Tom wrote down the letters as they came to him over the instruments. Suddenly he uttered a surprised whistle.

"Gee Whittaker!" he exclaimed in low tones. "Come here, Frank."

The other hurried to him and as he glanced at the pad on the table beside Tom he too gave an ejaculation of surprise. The letters which Tom had jotted down were as follows: LEAR P IN HAVANA ARRIVED YESTERDAY GET BUSY.

"They *are* rum runners!" cried Tom as the signals ceased.

"Gosh, I believe they are!" agreed Frank. "But of course," he added, "it may not mean your father by 'P' and we don't know the first part of the message. Maybe they were just talking about a ship—that 'lear' might have been something about a ship clearing for some place."

"You *are* a funny one," declared Tom. "Here you've been insisting all along that there was some deep mystery or plot behind these messages and I've said it was just some amateur and nothing to it and now, just as soon as we get a message which really means something, you shift around and say it's only about some boat."

"Well, if it's anything secret why do they talk plain English?" asked Frank. "That's what makes me change my views. When they were sending things that sounded like nonsense I thought they might be code messages, but now that they send things that are so plain it doesn't seem mysterious."

"Yes, there's sense in that argument, I admit," replied Tom. "But perhaps there was just as much sense in the others—if they *are* bootleggers. Of course as you say, they may not mean anything about Dad, but it would be a mighty funny coincidence if any one or anything else beginning with 'P' arrived in Havana yesterday and it happened to come in with this message and with a 'get busy' after it. I'll bet you, Frank, they're smugglers and that's a message to some boat or something that the coast's clear and to unload their stuff. Let's go down and tell Mr. Henderson about it."

"No," Frank advised. "He'd probably laugh at us and it wouldn't be any use to him anyhow. We'll keep the message and all others we hear and if anything else is going on we'll get some more messages, you can bet. And I've a scheme, Tom. I know a fellow down at Gramercy Park and we can go down there and set up a loop aërial and see if this chap that's talking is still southeast of there."

"That's a bully scheme!" cried Tom with enthusiasm. "We can turn radio detectives—that'll be great! And if we find he's north or west or east of Gramercy Square we can try some other place. Probably your friend knows fellows who have sets all around that part of the city."

The next day they visited Frank's friend and after making him promise secrecy they divulged a part of their plan, omitting, at Tom's suggestion, any reference to their suspicions of the messages coming from a gang of bootleggers. Henry fell in readily with the idea of locating the messages, which he had also heard repeatedly, and was deeply interested in the loop aërial. He had an excellent set and numerous instruments and supplies and the three boys soon rigged up a compass set in Henry's home.

"Now, you listen with this and try to pick him up," instructed Frank. "Keep turning the aërial about in this way and, as soon as you hear him, write down what he says. We'll listen too, whenever we have a chance, and will let you know. Then, if you haven't picked him up, you can turn the loop until you do. Too bad you haven't a sending set so you could tell us."

"But he'll hear you and quit," objected Henry, "and how can I hear you if I don't happen to have the loop pointed your way or am listening to this fellow?"

Frank looked puzzled. "Gee!" he ejaculated, "I hadn't thought of that.

"Oh, that's easy," declared Tom. "You'll hear us over the other set with the loud-speaker you have. That works with a regular aërial and is entirely separate from this set. And we'll arrange a code so he won't know what we're talking about. Let's see, I guess we'd better use the phone and not send dot and dash, we'll just say 'we've got the message' and you'll know what it means."

"No, that's no good," declared Frank. "That's not a bit mysterious or exciting. We're radio detectives, you know. We must have something like a password or code or something. Say, let's begin with 'loop,' then Henry'll know we mean him. We'll say 'loop, be ready to receive.'"

"Yes, and have him know something's wrong when we don't begin to send anything," said Tom.

"I have it!" exclaimed Henry, "Say, 'loop, coming over,' and then any one'll think you are telling me you are coming over here. But say, how'll I get your message if I don't sit at my set and tune to you?"

"That's easy," said Frank. "Just as soon as we get home to Tom's we'll begin to send and you listen and tune until you get us good and loud and then mark your knobs so you can set 'em whenever you want to hear us. Then ring us by regular phone and tell us it's O. K."

Thus, all being arranged, Tom and Frank went up town and as soon as they reached Tom's room began to send calls for Henry as they had agreed. Very soon the telephone bell rang and Tom ran to the instrument.

"It's all right, Frank," he announced as he returned to the room. "Henry says he got our calls finely and has marked his knobs. He's going to turn them about and then set them back at the marks and we're to call him again. Then if he gets us right off he'll know he won't miss us next time."

When, a few minutes later, the phone rang again and Henry told Tom that the message had come in on the adjusted set the boys felt sure that their fellow conspirator would not miss any calls they might send him. So, having nothing else to do, they worked at another step of amplification for their new set, and listened for any signals or messages that might come in from the person whom they were endeavoring to trail by means of radio.

Evidently, however, the mysterious stranger had no business to transact and no message from him was received. When at last they were obliged to leave for dinner they phoned to Henry who reported that he had been listening all the afternoon, but had heard nothing.

"We'll get at it again to-night," said Tom. "Most of the messages we've heard come in just when the broadcasting stations are giving their concerts. I'd bet he takes that time so nobody will hear him, or pay attention to him. If they're all tuned to 360 meters they'd never know he was talking, you see, and if they just chanced to hear him they'd be too busy with the music to bother with him."

As Tom had suspected, the mysterious messages did come in that night and so interesting and exciting did they prove to the boys' imaginative and suspicious minds that they were thankful they had foregone the pleasure of hearing the concert on the chance of the supposed smugglers talking.

CHAPTER III—THE RADIO DETECTIVES

The instant the boys recognized the long-awaited signals, Frank called Henry and notified him as agreed and, to their delight and satisfaction, the mysterious stranger continued to talk, evidently paying no heed to the seemingly innocent words of the boys, if indeed he had heard them.

As heretofore, much that was said meant nothing to the boys, but wisely they jotted every thing down nevertheless. However, both Tom and Frank were more puzzled than ever, for now that their minds were concentrated on the messages they suddenly realized that a true conversation, an interchange of messages, was going on, but, for some inexplicable reason, they could hear but one of the speakers. It was like listening to one individual talking to another over an ordinary telephone and the boys could merely guess at the words of the inaudible speaker.

"Yes, it's all right," came the words on the easily recognized short waves, "thirty-eight fifty seventy-seven; yes, that's it. Still there. Gave them the ha, ha! Azalia. Can't get anything on her. How about Colon? French Islands? Sure, they're just about crazy. No, no fear of that. Good stuff. No, no rough stuff. Expect her at same place about the tenth. No, don't hang around. Cleared the third. Fifteen seconds west. I'll tell him. Good bottom. Good luck! Don't worry, we'll see to that. No risk. So long!"

As the conversation ceased Tom jumped up. "Gee!" he exclaimed. "That's the most we've heard yet. I wonder if Henry got it."

Hurrying to the telephone, he was about to call Henry when the bell tinkled. "Hello!"—came the greeting in Henry's voice as Tom took down the receiver. "This is Henry. Say, did you get it?"

"You bet we did!" Tom assured him gleefully. "What did you make out? No, guess you'd better not tell over the phone. We'll be down there right away."

"He's east of here," declared Henry, when Tom and Frank reached his home.

"Golly, he must be in Brooklyn or out on the river!" exclaimed Tom. "What did you make out that he said?"

Henry showed them the message as he had jotted it down and which, with the exception of one or two words, was identical with what they had heard.

"I couldn't catch some of the words," explained Henry. "There was a funny sort of noise—like some one talking through a comb with paper on it,—the way we used to do when we were little kids—say, what's it all about anyway?"

"We don't know," replied Frank. "Did you hear any one else talking or anything?"

"And, Henry, were the sounds weak or faint to you?" put in Tom.

"Only that queer sound I told you about. The words were fine and strong here."

"Then he's nearer here than he is to us," announced Tom. "But I would like to know who the other fellow was and what he said and why the dickens we can't hear him when we hear this chap. Couldn't you make out any of the words that the fellow said—those that sounded like talking through a comb, I mean?"

"No, they were just a sort of buzzy mumble," replied Henry.

"Well if he's east of here it ought to be easy to locate him," remarked Frank. "Do you know any fellows around here who have sets, Henry?"

"Sure there are lots of 'em," Henry assured him. "Tom Fleming over at Bellevue has a dandy set and there's 'Pink' Bradley down on 19th St., and Billy Fletcher up on Lexington

Ave., and a whole crowd I don't know."

"Well, let's try it out at Fleming's place next, then," cried Frank. "Do you s'pose you can see him to-morrow and tell him the scheme? And say, ask him if he's heard the same talk."

"I can phone over to him now—I guess he's home," said Henry, "but what's back of all this? You fellows aren't so keen just because you want to locate this fellow that's been talking, I'll bet."

Tom hesitated, but in a moment his mind was made up.

"I suppose we might just as well tell you," he said at last. "But it's a secret and you'll have to promise not to tell any one else."

Henry readily agreed and Tom and Frank told him all they knew and what they suspected.

"Whew!" ejaculated Henry. "I shouldn't be surprised if you're right. I couldn't see any sense to all that talk about boats and the West Indies and numbers, but I can now. I'll bet those numbers were places out at sea—fifteen seconds west—and 'Azalia' may be the name of the ship. Say, won't it be bully if we can find out something—radio detectives—Gee, that's great!"

"Well, go on and call up Fleming," said Frank. "Tell him to come over here."

"He's on the way now," Henry announced when he returned to the room. "Are you fellows going to let him in on the bootlegger stuff?"

"Better not," advised Tom. "If he's heard the fellow talking we can tell him we're just anxious to locate him. We can make a mystery out of not hearing the person that was talking back, you know."

"It's a mystery all right enough," put in Frank. "If that other chap can hear him, why can't we? There's something mighty queer about it."

"Search me," replied Tom laconically. "Maybe he talks on a different wave length."

"I never thought of that," admitted Frank. "Say, next time they're talking one of us will listen while the other tunes to try and pick up the other man."

"And perhaps he's in a different direction," suggested Henry. "If he is of course we wouldn't hear him with our loops pointed towards this fellow."

"Of course!" agreed Tom. "We *have* been boobs. Just as like as not the one we didn't hear is over to the west or the north and we were all listening to the southeast. Say, you've got sense, old man. Next time we hear this chap we'll nab the other one, I bet. Hello! There's the bell."

Henry hurried from the room and returned presently, accompanied by another boy whom he introduced as Jim Fleming. Jim was undersized and round-shouldered with damp, reddish hair and big blue eyes behind horn-rimmed glasses. He had a most disconcerting manner of staring at one and constantly blinking and gulping—like a dying fish Frank declared later—and his hands and wrists seemed far too long for his sleeves. He was such a queer, gawky-looking chap that the boys could scarcely resist laughing, but before they had talked with him five minutes they had taken a great fancy to him and found he knew a lot about radio.

While the boys told him of their interest in the strange conversations, he stood listening, his long arms dangling at his sides, his big eyes blinking and his half-open mouth gulping spasmodically until Tom became absolutely fascinated watching him.

Mentally, Frank and Tom had dubbed him a "freak," a "simp," a "bookworm" and half a dozen far from complimentary names and they had expected to hear him speak "like a professor," as Tom would have expressed it. Instead he uttered a yell like a wild Indian, danced an impromptu jig and to the boys' amazement exclaimed:

"Hully Gee! So youse's onto that boid too! Say, fellers, isn't he the candy kid though? Spielin' on that flapper wave an' cannin' his gab if youse ask his call. Say, that boid oughter be up to the flooey ward—he's bughouse I'll say, with all his ship talk and numbers jazzed up an' chinnin' to himself. Say, did youse ever hear a bloke talkin' to him?"

"No, we never did," replied Tom. "Did you?"

"Nix!" answered Jim. "That's why I say he's got rats in his garret—flooey I'll say—" Then, suddenly dropping his slangy East Side expressions, he continued: "Say, he's had me guessing, too. But I can tell you one thing. He's west of my place—I'm over at Bellevue, you know—Dad's stationed there—and that'll bring him somewhere between East 27th St. and Gramercy Square."

"But, how on earth do you know that?" queried Tom in surprise.

Jim grinned and blinked.

"Same way you found out he was east of here," he replied. "You needn't think you fellows have got any patent on a loop, I've been usin' one for six months. Ed—he's my brother—is 'Sparks' on a big liner and showed me about it. But honest, if that fellow isn't crazy an' talkin' to himself, why don't we get the other guy sometimes?"

"That's the mystery to us," said Frank. "We decided just before you came in that the other fellow must be sending on a different wave length or else was in some other direction. We were just planning to pick him up by one of us tuning and turning the loop while the others listened to this fellow, but if you hear this man west of your place that knocks one of our theories out. If the other chap was west you'd get him, too."

"Yep, and 'tisn't because he's on a different length," declared Jim. "Hully Gee, I've tuned everywhere from 1500 meters down trying to get him, and nothin' doin'."

"Didn't you ever hear a funny sound like talking through a comb with paper on it?" asked Henry.

"Sure, sometimes I do," admitted Jim, "but you can't bring it in as chatter—I put it down to induction or somethin'—but Gee, come to think of it, it always does come in just right between this looney's sentences."

"I'll bet 'tis the other fellow," declared Henry. "Only if 'tis he's got an awful wheeze in his throat or his transmitter's cracked."

"Well, let's drop that and plan how we can locate this fellow we do hear," suggested Frank.

"Yes, now we know he's between your place and here we ought to find some place where we can set up a loop to the north and south," said Tom.

"Sure, we can fix that," declared Jim. "I've got a cousin that lives over on 23d St. and there's a good scout named Lathrop over on 26th. We can take sets to their places and put 'em up. They haven't anything but crystal sets, and most likely they'll know other guys and by trying out at different places we can spot his hangout all right. But say, what are you fellows so keen about findin' him for?"

"Oh, nothing except the fun of it," replied Tom, trying to act and speak in a casual manner. "You see we're just experimenting to find out what we can do with loop aërials—call ourselves radio detectives—and we picked on this fellow because his messages seemed sort of mysterious and are so easily recognized."

"Yea, I understand," said Jim. "Say that's a lulu of an idea— radio detectives. Well, I'll bet we can detect this bughousey guy O. K."

It was soon arranged that Jim was to see his cousin and that one of the boys' loops would be set up in his home the following evening and that, while Jim and Frank listened there, Henry and Tom would be at their sets and would call out as soon as they heard the messages from the mysterious speaker. All was arranged, but to the boys' intense chagrin not a sound came to any of them which remotely resembled the well-known voice and short wave lengths of the man they were striving to locate. But they were not discouraged, for they knew from past experience that they could not expect to hear him every night.

The following day was Saturday and the boys devoted their holiday to putting up a set in Lathrop's home. They now had four loop aërial sets ready to receive and located within a comparatively small area. They were sure that the station they were trying to find was within the few blocks between 20th and 27th Sts., but they were not at all sure whether it would be found to the east or west of Third Avenue. Moreover, as Jim pointed out, for all they knew he might be on 27th St. or 20th St. or even slightly north or south of one or the other, for he stated that his brother had told him that when close to a sending station the loop aërial could not be depended upon to give very accurate directions and that only by taking cross bearings could a certain point be definitely located. This was exactly what the boys had in view, to take cross bearings, and then, by means of a map of the city, to locate the man or the station.

It may seem as if the boys were devoting a great deal of time and trouble to something of little importance, but they were, or at least Tom, Frank and Henry were, thoroughly convinced that the messages emanated from some one connected with a rum-running gang and they were as keen on finding his location and as interested as if they had been real detectives detailed to discover a fugitive from justice.

So on that Saturday night they sat at their various instruments, waiting expectantly and with high hopes. No one was stationed at Tom's home, for, in order to provide two sets for the test, Tom's and Frank's had been dismantled and reinstalled at the houses of Jim's cousin and of Paul Lathrop.

Henry was the first to pick up the sounds and instantly he hurried to the telephone and called Jim. But by the time he had Jim's number the latter had also picked up the signals and had called the others, for Tom had not disturbed his transmission set and ordinary phoning was the only means of communicating with one another at the boys' disposal. For some time Tom, at the 23d St. house, could not pick up the sounds, but at last, with his loop pointed to the northeast, they came clear. "Congratulations," was the first word he heard, instantly followed by the queer buzzing sound which Henry had described. "Golly, 'tis just like some one talking through a comb," was Tom's mental comment and deeply interested and tremendously puzzled he strained his ears and mind striving to formulate words or meanings from the strange sounds. Once or twice he was sure that the sounds were words—he thought he could make out "last night" following a query of "When was it?" from the other speaker but, as he told the others later, it was like trying to hear what a mosquito was saying.

So intent was he on this that he quite forgot to jot down the plain words of the other speaker and did not realize it until the sounds ceased and the conversation was over.

But he knew that the others would have it and he had the direction, which was the main thing, and, a few minutes later all the boys were together and eagerly discussing the results of their experiment.

"He's southeast of my set!" announced Frank, when Tom had told them what he had discovered. "That puts him in between the river front and Third Avenue and between 23d and 26th Sts."

"Well, we're getting him narrowed down to a few blocks now," said Henry joyfully. "Say, what did you fellows make of the talk? Here's my slip."

The words that Henry had written down were as follows: "Everything O. K. Yes, haven't an idea. Sure, Fritz told me about it. Must be careful. No, but price will drop. No use killing the goose, you know. Golden eggs is right. Not a chance in the world of their getting wise. Nonsense, no one else has anything like it. Amateurs. Oh, forget it. Well, let 'em guess, guesses don't prove anything. Well, if they did they'd never find anything. Magnolia. Yes, same place thirty fifteen west. Oh, yes, the French stuff went like hot cakes. Sure, get all you can. Yes she cleared. Regards to Heinrich. Expect you the eighteenth. Don't forget Magnolia. Good-by."

"It's just the same as I made it," announced Frank.

"Same here," said Jim. "Sufferin' cats! Do you mean to say that nut isn't bughouse now?"

"It *does* sound a bit crazy, I admit," replied Tom. "Say, did any of you fellows try tuning to different wave lengths to see if any one else came in?"

"I did," declared Frank, "but all I got was some one who said 'for the love of Mike get off the air.'"

"Me, too," chimed in Jim. "No one's talking to him, he's just nutty and chins to himself."

"Well, then, we have all the more reason for finding him," said Tom. "If he's really crazy the authorities ought to know it. Now we know he's so close we ought to be able to locate him."

So, day after day, the boys, their interest and enthusiasm at high pitch owing to the success of their experiments, shifted their instruments from house to house, gradually drawing their radio net about the mysterious sender until they were positive that he was located in a certain block, a district of small, old-fashioned buildings, warehouses and garages.

But beyond this they could not go. There were no boys so far as they knew within the area and, satisfied that they had done all they could and that they had proved the value of their loops in locating the unknown speaker, all but Tom, Frank and Henry lost interest and devoted their attention to other matters.

But Tom, Frank, and, to a lesser degree, Henry were still deeply interested in the mysterious messages and were convinced that they came either from a gang of rum-runners or from some other law-breakers, for while there was nothing really suspicious in the messages they could not rid themselves of the idea, once it had entered their minds.

"I vote we go and tell Mr. Henderson all we know," said Tom. "Dad won't be back for two weeks or more yet and if Mr. Henderson thinks there's anything in it he can have that block searched and find out who owns the set."

"Well, perhaps 'twould be a good plan," admitted Frank, and accordingly the two boys went to Mr. Henderson's office and related the story of their experiments and told of their suspicions.

"H-m-m," remarked the keen-eyed man when they had ended, "this is very interesting, boys. Let me see the notes you made."

For a time he examined the slips of paper bearing the various messages the boys had scribbled down and his forehead wrinkled in a frown of perplexity.

"It's very indefinite," he announced at last, half to himself, "but I agree with you that the whole matter has a suspicious appearance. Too bad you didn't take down the earlier messages you heard. Now, let's see. You say you have never heard the other party to the conversations and yet you have been listening in within a block of this chap. Very odd, yes, most extraordinary. There are several explanations that occur to me, however. For example, if they wished the conversation to be secret and unintelligible they might have arranged that one man was to talk through an ordinary phone and the other by radio. Or they might have arranged this because the second man had no sending set—exactly as you boys communicated with one another with only one transmission set among you."

"Gee, but we *are* dumb-bells!" exclaimed Tom. "Why the dickens didn't we think of that? Why we are doing the same thing ourselves. It was so simple we overlooked it."

Mr. Henderson smiled. "That's often the way," he declared. "During the war a lot of messages passed our censors as perfectly innocent and harmless and yet they were of the utmost importance—they were so frank and simple we overshot the mark."

"Yes, Dad told us about some of those," said Tom.

"As I was saying," went on Mr. Henderson, "if one man was talking over a telephone you would not have heard him under ordinary conditions, but it often happens that through capacity inductance a phone message may come in over a radio set. That might account for your occasionally hearing those sounds which you describe as resembling words coming through a paper-covered comb. Do you remember the conditions under which you heard those sounds? Were you near telephone receivers, touching any part of your sets or doing anything unusual?"

The boys thought deeply, trying to revisualize the conditions that had existed on the few occasions when they had heard the odd buzzing sounds.

"I'm not sure," said Tom at last, "but it seems to me that when I heard them the first time—that time I was on 23d St., I was sitting close to the telephone receiver on the table—I'd just been called up by Jim and—yes, I am sure now, I remember distinctly—I had my hand touching the stand while I was listening to the messages. You see, I was half inclined to phone to the others to find out if they heard the sounds and I reached out to pick up the phone and then changed my mind—but sort of kept my hand there."

"Then that's solved, I think," declared Mr. Henderson. "If you had taken down the phone receiver and had kept your hand upon it you would probably have heard the other speaker's voice plainly."

"Gosh, why didn't we think of that!" interrupted Frank. "And come to think of it, the phone *is* on the same table with the radio set at Henry's house."

"Well, we've laid one ghost, we'll assume," went on Mr. Henderson, "but that does not solve the mystery of the other speaker nor does it eliminate the possibility that these fellows may be crooks. In our work, you know, we always assume that every suspect is guilty until we prove our theory wrong and so we'll assume that your mysterious speaker is a crook until we find we're mistaken. However, before I take any active steps I think it will be a good plan to try another test. Suppose you listen in for a few nights more and, as soon as you hear this fellow, take down your phone receivers and hold the instrument against your body or arm and see if you get the voice of the other chap. Let me know the results and then we can plan our next move."

"Hurrah! Now we *are* real radio detectives working for the government!" cried Tom enthusiastically. "Do you really think they're bootleggers?"

"I make it a point never to form a hard-and-fast opinion," replied Mr. Henderson with a smile at the boys' excitement. "However, I should not be in the least surprised if they are, and if so and we round them up, Uncle Sam will have to thank you boys. Go to it, boys! Perhaps we may have to organize a radio detective corps yet, and I'm not sure that boys may not be able to show us old hands a few tricks at our own game."

CHAPTER IV—THE BOYS DRAW A BLANK

Hardly had the door to Mr. Henderson's office closed behind them before Frank commenced to dance and caper wildly about.

"Hurrah!" he shouted. "This *is* great! We're real detectives and working for Uncle Sam!"

"Yes, but don't make such a row," cautioned Tom. "We don't want every one in the place to know it and they'll think you're crazy. Come on, let's hurry and tell Henry."

When they reached Gramercy Square and dashed into Henry's room and told him of their talk with Mr. Henderson, he was as excited and pleased as Frank.

"Say, it *was* funny we didn't think of that fellow using a telephone!" he exclaimed, when the boys had told him of Mr. Henderson's theory. "And he's right about that capacity effect of a fellow near a phone. I *was* a fool not to have thought of it. Why, Jim told me about that long ago. He even said his brother Ed showed him with his set on the *San Jacinto*. But I guess it must have been because we were so intent on the messages that we couldn't think of anything else. I'll bet we can hear folks on the phone through my set right now."

"That *is* funny!" declared Tom, when, a moment later, the boys were listening to a telephone conversation coming to them through Henry's set. "Say," he continued, "there isn't much privacy nowadays, is there? Why, if you could amplify that enough, every one could hear everything that was going on over the telephones."

"Yes, and to think we were so close to getting that other chap's talk and never realized it," said Frank. "Mr. Henderson must think we are great radio fans! I'll bet he had a mighty good laugh at our expense after we left."

"Well, we'll not be fooled again," declared Tom. "If that fellow begins talking to-night we'll nail him, too."

"But we can't locate him," objected Henry. "So what good will it do?"

"That's so," admitted Tom. "But the main thing is to hear what he says. Then perhaps we can make sense out of it."

"Say," suddenly exclaimed Henry, "did you fellows notice that every time we heard those messages the fellow mentioned a flower? First 'twas 'Azalia' and then 'Magnolia' and then 'Hibiscus' and last time 'twas 'Frangi Pani.' I'd like to know what that meant."

"I hadn't thought of that," said Tom. "Of course Azalia and Magnolia and Hibiscus are flowers, but what's Frangi Pani— sounds like some sort of Japanese thing to me. I guess this fellow must be talking about boats. Lots of ships are named after flowers, you know."

"Well, he must have a whole fleet then," said Henry.

"Perhaps it's perfumes or he may be in the flower business," suggested Frank with a laugh.

"Perhaps we'll get the answer to that when we hear his mate," said Tom.

"Hope we hear him to-night," remarked Henry. "Say, what do you think of this scheme?"

For some time the boys forgot all else in examining a new hook-up which Henry had devised and at last left him with final cautions to be at his instruments that evening and each night thereafter until they again heard the unknown speakers.

But it was several nights before the mysterious messages again greeted their ears. Then Frank and Tom caught them at the same instant and both boys gave a little start and looked at each other in surprise, for the first word they heard was "Tuberose." Once more the name of a flower had entered into the conversation and mentally wondering what in the world this meant the two boys slipped the receiver of the desk telephone from its hook. Hardly had they done so when they almost jumped, as clear and loud, they heard a human voice; but the next instant their spirits sank to zero and they glanced at each other with disgusted expressions, for instead of the voice of the man they had expected to hear they heard a woman's voice and her words were: "Number, please?"

With a savage jerk, Tom hung up the receiver.

"Gee!" he exclaimed. "Of course we'd get *her*. I'll bet Mr. Henderson knew that and just tried to jolly us. Now what *are* we going to do? If we—Hello! What's that?"

Clearly to his ears, and interrupting the words of the mysterious man whom they had almost forgotten in their disappointment, came another voice, evidently that of a woman, and pitched in high tones. "Oh, yes!" it exclaimed. "I'm *so* glad, my dear. Do you know—" Tom drew his hand from the desk phone on which it had been resting and the words trailed off into a faint indistinct buzz. Tom and Frank grinned.

"Well, it works!" ejaculated Frank. "Of course it doesn't make any difference if the receiver is off or not—we aren't getting waves over wires. Henry kept the receiver on to-day, didn't he?"

"I don't know," replied Tom. "But say, we've got to get busy. That chap's been talking for the last five minutes and we haven't put down a thing he's said."

Trying to make up for lost time, the two boys jotted down the words that came in, now and then placing a hand on the desk phone to see if they could hear the other party to the conversation, but each time the nasal voice of the woman, gossiping with a friend, was all that came to them. Then the man's voice ceased and after a few moments' wait the boys rose from their seats.

"Darn that old hen!" exclaimed Tom, petulantly. "How the dickens could a fellow expect to hear anything with her tongue going like a house afire?"

"Just think what it'll be when every one's talking by radio," chuckled Frank. "And won't the women have the time of their lives hearing all their neighbors' gossip?"

"Government'll have to license 'em to talk, I guess," muttered Tom. "Come on, let's go over to Henry's and see if he had any better luck."

But Henry had nothing to tell them. He had heard no conversation over the phone except some man talking business with a friend, but he had written down all the words the mysterious man had spoken and showed them to the boys who had explained how they had forgotten to get the greater part of the conversation.

"Tuberose," Tom read. "We'll begin next week. Getting stocked up. I'll bet it'll wake things up. Too bad we didn't know then. Might have been a different tale, eh? Oh, Oscar's all right. Yes, same old place. Nothing doing, old man. Never a suspicion. Oh, it's a cinch. I don't know. Some kids, I expect. Got to see him to-night. So long, old man."

"Just the same old stuff," commented Tom when he had finished. "Only no figures this time."

"And another flower," added Henry.

"Jim would swear he was crazy if he noticed that," chuckled Frank. "I'm beginning to think that may be it myself."

For three consecutive nights the boys heard the conversation and despite all efforts failed to hear anything of interest over the ordinary phones while the radio words were coming in, although they heard various scraps of conversations between other persons.

"Mr. Henderson was off that time," declared Tom, when the boys rose from their sets on the third night. "His theory was wrong. The other chap's not talking on a telephone, I'll bet."

"Doesn't look that way at any rate," agreed Frank. "Let's go down to-morrow and tell him."

Accordingly, the three boys visited Mr. Henderson the next day and reported the results of their experiments.

"That *does* puzzle me," exclaimed Mr. Henderson as they finished. "If you heard others it's pretty conclusive evidence he's not on a wire. Did you hear those buzzing sounds or words again?"

"I did," said Henry, "and I heard 'em just as plain and no plainer when I was a long way from the phone as when I was touching it."

"Well, we've drawn a blank there," smiled Mr. Henderson. Then, after a moment's thought, he exclaimed, "Boys, I'm going to take a chance. I'm pretty well convinced something's going on that's crooked and I'm going to send some men out and search every building in that block from cellar to garret. You understand, of course, this is a profound secret. No one will know who they are or what they're after. It must be a surprise visit so don't even talk it over among yourselves. But I want you to help us a bit. I'm going to start the men out at eight o'clock sharp, to-night. You must be at your sets and listening. If the fellow's talking, you'll know when my men find him, either by what he says or the way he shuts off, and if he goes on talking without interruption for half an hour you'll know you've made some mistake and he's not in that block. Meet me here to-morrow at about this time and we'll have something to report—or nothing."

"Oh, and there's something else," announced Tom as the boys turned to leave. "Henry called attention to those names of flowers yesterday. We'd almost forgotten about them. Every time that fellow talks he gets a new name of a flower. Have you noticed it?"

Mr. Henderson chuckled. "You're getting a pretty good training at this, boys," he replied. "Yes, I've noticed that—that's one thing that influences me more than anything else. There's some code to those names, I think, and they may prove the key to the whole thing. We'll find out sometime probably."

Remembering Mr. Henderson's injunction about discussing the proposed raid the boys refrained from mentioning it to one another, but could scarcely restrain their impatience until the time came for them to be at their instruments.

Eight o'clock came and, excited and expectant, the boys listened, hoping to hear the message coming in and to learn from its words or its abrupt ending of the success of the raid. But the minutes ticked by, the hands of the clock pointed to half-past eight, and nine o'clock came and went without a word from the source they so longed to hear.

Anxious to learn the result of the search, the boys hurried to Mr. Henderson's office the following day.

"Another blank, boys," he announced when they entered his office. "There wasn't a sign of a wireless outfit in that block. Did you hear anything last night?"

The boys admitted that they had heard nothing.

"But—but there *must* be a set there," insisted Tom, utterly unable to believe that they had been mistaken. "Why, we were all around there with our loops and we got cross bearings and knew he was there."

"It's a bit mysterious, I grant," replied Mr. Henderson. "I

fully expected we'd locate it, but my men will swear there isn't even a piece of radio apparatus in the block. They went through it with a fine-tooth comb. Either you boys were mistaken or else the fellow's moved away. If you hear him again you'll know whether he's changed his location. I'm afraid you'll never locate him by your instruments, though. I've used those loops as direction finders at sea and to some extent ashore and I admit I can't see how you went wrong, but we've got to face the fact that he's not there—at least not now."

Thoroughly disappointed and discouraged, the boys left the office and for hours discussed the matter with one another, but at the end of the time were no nearer a solution than ever.

"Oh, bother the old thing, anyhow!" exclaimed Tom at last. "We've had our fun and now let's do something else. Dad's leaving Nassau to-morrow and we can try sending to him when he gets nearer. Wonder what he'll say about this thing."

"Yes, but it gets my goat to think that Mr. Henderson will think we're such dubs," said Frank. "He thinks we've made some big mistake and put him to all that trouble for nothing."

"Well, let's forget it," suggested Henry, and this seeming the best advice the boys followed it and were soon so busy experimenting along new lines that the mysterious conversations almost slipped from their minds, and as no further messages were heard from the same source they decided that by some coincidence the sender had moved bag and baggage from his former location just in time to escape detection by the men Mr. Henderson had sent on the search.

Tom and Frank were overjoyed when, a day before Mr. Pauling's ship docked, they succeeded in getting a message to him.

"That's pretty near 300 miles," declared Tom jubilantly, "and our set's only supposed to send 100. Say, that's a real freak message."

But when, a few moments later, they heard some one calling

their letters and this was followed by a question as to their location and the information that the inquirer was the government operator at Fort Randolph, Canal Zone, Panama, the two boys could only stare at each other in utter amazement.

"Jehoshaphat!" exclaimed Frank at last. "We were heard clear down in Panama! Why that's pretty near 2000 miles!"

"Almost as good as that fellow over in Jersey who was heard in Scotland and Honduras!" cried Tom. "Hurrah, Frank! Let's try again."

But despite every effort the boys failed to get a reply from any one more than fifty or sixty miles distant and realized that, by some peculiar atmospheric condition, their dots and dashes had been carried through the ether for twenty times and more their normal sending range.

"That's something to tell Dad," declared Tom, and rushing down the stairs he excitedly told his mother of the wonderful feat.

"I suppose it is remarkable, if you say so," said Mrs. Pauling, "but really, I can't see why you should not talk to Balboa or Europe or any other point if you can talk to your father's ship out at sea. One is just as wonderful as the other to me. But I'm proud of you just the same, Tom."

When, the next day, Mr. Pauling arrived, Tom could scarcely wait to relate the story of his freak message and his father was enthusiastic enough to satisfy any boy.

"Marvelous!" he declared. "And the operator on the *San Jacinto* tells me you've improved a lot since he first talked to you. Says you can send well and had no trouble in getting his message at regular speed. I'm mighty glad you've done so well, Son. Just as soon as I have a chance I'm coming up to see that wonder set of yours. How many have you built since I've been gone?"

Then Tom told his father of the mysterious messages and what had come of their attempts to locate the sender.

Mr. Pauling laughed heartily. "Well, if you got old Henderson interested he must have believed there was something in it. I don't know but what there was. I'll talk it over with him. But I can imagine your disappointment, and his too—when nothing came of it. No, Son, I can't offer any explanation and we're as much in the dark as ever about the smugglers. By the way, I met a chap down at Nassau that was just about as keen on experiments as you boys only he's not a radio fan. No, he's a diver. He's invented a new type of diving suit—self-contained he calls it. Just a sort of rubber cloth shirt and a khaki-colored helmet and lead-soled shoes. He goes down without ropes or life lines or air hose. Gets his air from a little box or receptacle strapped to his body. I don't know what is in it, but it's some chemical which produces oxygen and he can walk about where he pleases on the bottom. It's the weirdest thing I've ever seen to watch him wade out into the water and disappear and then, half an hour or two hours later, have him bob up somewhere else."

"Gosh, I'd love to see that," declared Tom. "Suppose he wants to come up from deep water without walking ashore, how does he manage?"

"He just produces more oxygen so he floats up," replied Mr. Pauling. "And you'll have a chance to talk with him next week. He's returning to New York and I've asked him to call and see us. Nice young chap, name's Rawlins. The only trouble with his outfit is that he can't communicate with others ashore or on the boats. Of course he can take down a line or even a telephone, but then he at once destroys one of the great advantages of his invention. A trailing line or wire is as liable to be caught or tangled in a wreck or in coral as an air pipe or any other rope or line and it means some one must be stationed in a boat over him. He claims one big advantage of his suit will be the fact that as no boat or air pump is needed, no one can tell where he is. That would be a fine thing in time of war, of course. Think you'll take a great fancy to him, Tom."

For a moment, Tom was silent and then he suddenly let out a yell like an Indian.

"I have it!" he fairly screamed. "Radio! Submarine radio! I'll bet it'll work."

Then, filled with enthusiasm, he started to explain his ideas to his father.

"All right! All right!" cried Mr. Pauling, laughing and holding up his hands in protestation. "I'll take your word for the technical end of it. Wait and tell Rawlins about it. But honestly I don't know but what there may be something in it. You and Rawlins can work it out."

So filled with his new idea was Tom, that he fairly rushed to tell Frank when the latter arrived, and for the next ten days the two were ceaselessly at work, drawing plans and diagrams, making and discarding instruments, purchasing countless rolls of wire and knock-down apparatus, as they strove to put into concrete form the vision in Tom's brain.

But they found innumerable difficulties to be overcome and were almost discouraged when one evening Rawlins called.

He was such an enthusiastic and interesting man that the boys took a huge liking for him and as soon as Tom told him of his idea he at once fell in with the boys' plans.

"I do believe it can be done!" he declared, when Tom had shown him the plans and had described his ideas fully. "I don't know much about radio, but if you are right about the matter there's no reason I can see why you shouldn't get it to work. I tell you what, Tom, we'll fit up a workshop and laboratory down at my father's dock—it's down near the foot of 28th St. and we don't use it except for storage. The old gentleman's gone out of the wrecking business and has sold all his outfit except the things stored there. It's a fine place to work and experiment. There are tools and a machine lathe and about ten tons of odds and ends that may come in handy. My father had his office and workshop there—did all his repairing of pumps, diving suits and tugs there, and never threw anything away. I learned to dive there—my father and grandfather were deep-sea divers, too—and there's a trapdoor where the divers went down to test their suits and pumps. I made my suits and even my under-sea motion picture outfit there and it's private and no one will disturb us. The only way we can test out this idea of yours is by actual trial under water. If we do get it, it will be a mighty big thing—greatest improvement in sub-sea work ever. I'll get the place ready and cleaned up a bit to-morrow. I'm just as crazy as you are to try it out."

Mr. Henderson also was deeply interested in the boys' new experiments and declared he believed their ideas might be worked out successfully.

"You'll run across a lot of unexpected and unforeseen difficulties," he warned them. "One never knows what new laws and phenomena one may run up against in a thing of this sort. During the war our government and the Allies, and no doubt Germany also, carried on a good many experiments with under-water radio, but as far as I know they never came to much. Radio had not progressed so far then and there were more important things to be done and not enough men to attend to it. We *did* use vacuum tubes and amplifiers for detecting submarines, however. By the way, I have a few things that may be of help to you boys and I'll be glad to let you have them. Among them is a remarkable tuning device of German make and I don't think it has ever been tried out. You'll need something that is simple and accurate and easy to control and this may do the trick."

By the end of a week a snug little laboratory had been set up on Rawlins' dock and the boys and their diver friend spent every available moment of their time there.

Tom and Frank were as interested in seeing Rawlins go down in his odd suit as he was in their radio work, and the first time he put it on to demonstrate it to the boys they became tremendously excited. Rawlins carefully explained all about it, pointing out its various parts and showing them how the oxygen generator worked.

"You have to be careful about this," he said, "if a drop of water gets into it, it blazes or flames up and may kill a fellow. That's the only danger about it. If a man forgets and takes the mouthpiece from his lips to speak without shutting it off and water gets in, he'll have a red hot flame inside his helmet. It's easy to get accustomed to it though—comes as natural as breathing, after a bit of practice."

But even now that it had been explained to them it seemed a most remarkable feat for Rawlins to don the shirtlike suit and helmet and, with only these over his ordinary garments and with no rubber trousers covering his legs, descend the ladder and disappear in the water without lines, pipes or ropes trailing after him. Both Tom and Frank were crazy to go down, but Rawlins refused to permit it until he had made the suits "fool proof" as he put it. Even then, the boys' parents objected until they had visited the workshop and Rawlins had proved to their satisfaction that the boys were perfectly safe in shallow water when he accompanied them.

"We'll have to go down to test out the radio," argued Tom, "so we might as well learn right away."

At last the fathers gave in and Tom went down first with Rawlins. For a week afterwards he could think or talk of nothing else and never tired relating his sensations and experiences to his parents and his boy friends, and Frank did the same. But after the first few times the novelty wore off and the boys soon became quite accustomed to going to the bottom of the river. Rawlins, however, never allowed them to stay down more than a few minutes at a time and after the first few descents the boys found little fun in it. They had expected to find a smooth, hard bottom and to see fishes swimming about and to be able to look up and see passing boats overhead. To their surprise, they found they could not walk upright, but leaned far forward and had a peculiar dreamy sensation when they attempted to walk, their feet seeming to half-drag, half-float behind them and that, despite the fact that the bottom of the river was soft and muddy, they did not sink into the bottom to any extent. As Tom put it, it was like trying to hurry in a dream when one's feet seem tied to something and one can't possibly run. Moreover, they found the water dark and so filled with sediment that they could see but a few feet and even near-by objects, such as the spiles and abutments of the dock, the ladder down which they descended and the figure of their companion were scarcely visible a yard distant and took on strange, hazy, indistinct and distorted forms. Indeed, Rawlins always held their hands when they went down, explaining that should they stray a few yards away they might be lost or might be swept off in some current.

But they were glad of the experience and realized that in order to carry on their experiments with any hopes of success they must learn to use the suits, for Rawlins had not yet mastered the details of radio.

In the meantime, however, they worked at the radio devices and at last Tom announced that he had a set which he believed might work.

"It's only an experimental set," he explained to Rawlins. "And it won't stand up long under water, but if the idea's all right and we get any results we can go to work and make a good outfit on the same principle."

Rawlins was almost as excited as the boys when the day came to test the new device and at Tom's suggestion was to go down alone with the receiver in his helmet while the boys remained on the dock and attempted to communicate with him.

"We'll try receiving under water first," said Tom. "If it works we'll get it into good shape and then get busy on the under-water sending set."

So, with the compact but complicated little set inside his helmet, which was specially made to accommodate it, and with the receivers clamped over his ears, Rawlins backed down the ladder while the boys, feeling like explorers about to set foot on some new and unknown land, watched his head disappear beneath the surface of the river.

It was little wonder that they were wildly excited for now, in a few moments, they would know beyond question whether their ideas had been right and whether all their work and trouble had been thrown away or they had made an advance in radio which might revolutionize under-sea work.

At first the boys had not fully realized what the success of their efforts would mean and had gone into it enthusiastically merely as something new and strange.

But as soon as Rawlins had explained the possibilities which a successful under-sea radio telephone would open up, they understood how much might hinge on the triumph or failure of their plans.

"Why," Rawlins had exclaimed, "think what it will do if it works! A man can go down and walk about any place he chooses and yet can talk back and forth with men on a ship or on shore. In wrecking, he could go all through a ship with no danger of getting his life-line or air-hose tangled and he could direct the fellows on the tug or lighter, telling them just where to lower chains or tackle or anything else. And think what it would mean in time of war! Why, a man could walk out from shore anywhere, go under a ship and fasten a mine to her and blow her up and hear all that was going on aboard the enemy's ship. And just think what a dangerous sort of spy a man would be—out of sight under the sea and yet able to hear all the talk and messages of the enemy! I tell you, boys, up to now diving's been like blind man's work—mostly feeling and signaling by jerks on a line. Of course the ordinary phone was a big advance, but with that you still had to trail a wire along and there was a visible connection between the diver and the surface. With my suits and your radio the country that owned the secrets would be mighty near masters of the sea, I'll say."

CHAPTER V—THE UNDER-SEA WIRELESS

As soon as Rawlins was out of sight the boys commenced to talk, Tom speaking through the transmitter while Frank wrote down what he said, for of course they could not know if Rawlins heard them, and the only means of determining if he had received all the words was to keep a record for comparison when he came up. They were busily engaged at this and tremendously interested and excited, when the telephone bell rang. Telling Rawlins to wait a moment, and explaining the reason, Tom ceased speaking while Frank answered the call.

"Hello, Frank," came Henry's voice. "I just rang up to be sure you were there. How's everything going?"

"Fine!" replied Frank, "come on down, we're just testing it out for the first time. When did you get back?"

"Last evening—but didn't have a chance to run around to see you. I called up, but the maid said you were out with Tom. Didn't she tell you? I'll be right down, you bet. Say, I've some news for you. So long."

"I'm glad he's back from that trip with his father and is coming down," said Tom, "Won't he be interested and surprised if this works? Wonder what the news is."

Then, turning to his set, he continued his interrupted talk, or attempt to talk, with Rawlins until, five minutes later, Henry was pounding at the door.

"Gee, but you've a fine place here!" he cried as he glanced about the little laboratory, "and you've diving suits and helmets and everything. Say, I was just crazy to get back when I got your letter telling about your experiments and everything. Where's the diver fellow? Oh say, you're not really talking to him under water! Crickety! Isn't that wonderful to think he can hear you down under the river!"

Tom laughed. "Don't know if he can," he replied. "We'll have to wait for him to come up and tell. You see we haven't got an under-sea sending set rigged up yet and the one he's got is just a sort of makeshift for experimenting."

"Have you fellows heard anything more of that mystery chap?" cried Henry, suddenly changing the subject.

"Not a word," Tom assured him.

"Well, I have then," declared Henry triumphantly. "I heard him last night and I got him again to-day just before I called you fellows. He was in the same old place, too."

"Honest? Say, that *is* funny!" exclaimed Frank. "What was he saying?"

"Don't know," replied Henry, "He was talking some foreign lingo that I couldn't make out, but I got one word. Bet you couldn't guess what 'twas—another flower—Oleander this time."

The boys were so interested in Henry's news that they had temporarily forgotten their under-water companion until Henry uttered a half surprised exclamation and jumped away from the square opening in the floor over the river.

"Gosh, there he comes!" he cried, as overcoming his first surprise at a gurgling splash he glanced through the trapdoor and saw the diver's helmet appearing. "Don't he look like a regular sea monster?"

A moment later, Rawlins was removing his suit and helmet.

"Did you hear us?" cried Tom the moment Rawlins' face was visible.

"Did I!" exclaimed the diver. "Did I! Let me tell you I wished I had cotton stuffed in my ears. You must think I'm deaf,— yelling like that. Did you think you had to shout loud enough to have your voice go through the water? And I'll tell you I thought a tornado'd struck the place when your friend here arrived. I even heard the telephone bell."

Tom and Frank fairly danced with delight. "Hurrah! It works! It's a success! We've solved it! It's under-sea radio!" shouted the excited boys.

"I'll say it works!" declared Rawlins. "But what the deuce were you trying to talk Dutch for?"

"Talk Dutch?" cried Tom in a puzzled tone. "We weren't talking Dutch or anything but United States."

It was Rawlins' turn to be amazed. "Well, who in thunder was then?" he asked. "I heard some one jabbering Dutch or some other foreign language—don't know what 'twas except it wasn't French or Spanish."

Henry gave a whoop. "It was that other fellow!" he cried excitedly. "I'll bet 'twas. He was talking just before I rang up as I told you. Jehoshaphat! Mr. Rawlins must have heard him under water."

"I guess that's it," agreed Tom. "Funny it didn't occur to me. Of course there's no reason why he shouldn't have been heard under water. We're using a tiny little wave length and so's he, and he's close to here, you know. Did you hear him loudly, Mr. Rawlins?"

"Well, not so as to deafen me the way you did," replied the diver with a grin, "but if I'd understood his lingo I could have told what he was talking about. The only word that sounded like sense to me was something like Oleander."

"Then 'twas him!" fairly yelled Henry ungrammatically. "That's the name he was using when I heard him."

"Well, it just proves this new thing is a peacherino," declared Tom. "Now let's get busy and fix it up in good shape and make a sending set to try out."

Now that the boys' first experiment had been such a huge success they were more enthusiastic and excited than ever. They had been confident that the diver would be able to hear sounds or that he might even distinguish words under water, but they had not dared to hope that their very first efforts would result in the sound being carried to the ears of the man beneath the water as clearly and loudly as though he had been present in the same room with the speaker.

"I'll bet water carries electromagnetic waves better than air," declared Tom. "Why, if this little set can respond to these short five watt waves in this way, think what it would mean to a submarine with big amplified sets and getting messages sent with hundreds of watts. Why a fellow could sit in Washington and talk to submarines and divers all over the Atlantic."

"You've hit on a wonderful possibility," Rawlins assured him. "Of course I was pretty close—I didn't go over a hundred yards from the dock and it's shoal water. I'm anxious to try it down a hundred feet or so and a mile or two from the sender. We'll do that after we get things right—go down to my hangout in the Bahamas and give it a real honest-to-goodness tryout."

"It's all in that new amplifying arrangement and that single control tuner Frank hit upon," said Tom. "And we're not really responsible for either. Mr. Henderson gave us the idea for the tuner and a friend of Dad's invented the tube, but couldn't get any one interested. You see, Henry, this tube is just about 400 times as much of an amplifier as the other tubes, and we get a detector and amplifier all in one. Look here—it's the smallest bulb you ever saw—about the size of a peanut and we operate it on a flashlight battery with a special little dry cell for the filament. Of course they don't last long, but a fellow can't stay down more than an hour or two anyway and the batteries will run the set steadily for five hours. For under-sea work the cost don't count. What we're up against now is to make the sending set to go with it. The receiver was easy. That fits in this special helmet all right and don't have to be waterproof, but the sending set'll have to be outside and it'll be an awful job to keep the water from short circuiting it."

As he talked, Tom was showing Henry the set and pointing out its many novel features.

"This single tuner is great," he continued. "It's fixed so it's set at a certain spot for the normal wave lengths sent from the diver's home station. See, here in the middle at zero. Then, if he wants to get a shorter wave he turns it to the left which gives him a range down to half his normal wave length, or for longer waves he turns it to the right and gets twice his normal length. If he wants to go to long wave lengths—for example, if he was a spy or something and wanted to get the big sending stations— he'd turn the knob clear to the left and then back to the right and around to opposite the zero point. Then he'd be on about 2500 meters and that being his utmost length he just has to tune slowly towards zero again. And the rheostat works automatically with it and so does the variable condenser and it's not very complicated either."

"But what does he do for an aërial?" queried Henry.

"Doesn't use one," replied Tom. "Just has this sort of wire cage sticking from his helmet, like a loop, but made of two grids set at right angles to each other. But gosh! I never thought about there being interferences under water."

"I suppose Henry understands all that," interrupted Rawlins laughingly, "but it means about as much to me as that Dutch talk I heard. Somehow or other I can't get on to this radio a little bit. When you get that sending outfit rigged you'll have to go down and test it. I'd probably bungle something. I didn't even dare meddle with this gadget for tuning. I tried it once and when your voice stopped I just shoved her back and let it go at that. That's when I heard that Dutchman."

"Then he's on a different wave length and it proves *we* can tune out under water," declared Tom gleefully. "That's another feather in our caps."

Henry quickly grasped the boys' ideas and together the three worked diligently until sundown while Rawlins busied himself devising the fittings for his suit to accommodate the sending apparatus and helped the boys tremendously with suggestions for rendering a set watertight and with advice as to mechanical and other details.

By the time they were obliged to stop their work the plans for the under-sea transmission set were well worked out and, with high hopes and flushed with the success of their achievements, they locked up the workshop and walked up town discussing plans for the morrow.

The following day they went to the dock right after breakfast, for school was over for the season and they had all their time to themselves. Rawlins was already there and before they left that night they had the set nearly completed and Tom declared they would be able to give it a test the next day.

Mr. Pauling was of course deeply interested and enthusiastic over the boys' work and promised to go down himself as soon as the instruments were perfected. He listened to the boys' glowing accounts of their work and their success and later, when Mr. Henderson called, he too became most optimistic regarding their under-sea radio.

"It's merely a question of experimenting, boys," he declared. "We were on the right track during the war, but radio's jumped ahead a lot since then and whatever the government experts accomplish is kept mighty quiet. I'm glad that single control works out so well. We'll have to thank the Huns for that. We found one on a captured U-boat, but as far as I know the government never took it up seriously—don't know why unless it was because there was no particular need of it. We never did find out what the Germans used it for—for all we know they may have been experimenting along under-sea lines too. And if that new tube of Michelson's proves good he'll make a fortune and have you boys to thank for it. I'm coming down to see your outfit just as soon as we get a breathing space. We're rushed to death just now."

With nothing else to do the boys amused themselves listening at their sets which, with so many other interests, had been sadly neglected of late, and, out of pure curiosity and never expecting to hear anything, Tom turned his loop aërial to the southeast and tuned for the short wave lengths used by the mysterious talker they had once followed and tried to locate so persistently. To his surprise, the sound of words came clearly over the set.

"There he is again!" Tom exclaimed to Frank who was listening to a broadcasted speech. "Get him and we'll see what he says."

But despite the fact that the boys could both hear the man plainly his words were meaningless, for he was speaking some guttural, harsh-sounding tongue.

"Oh, pshaw!" ejaculated Tom disgustedly after a few minutes of this. "Who cares what he's saying. I guess it's some crazy foreigner."

So saying, he again picked up the broadcasting station and forgot all about the incident in his interest as he listened to a lecture on new developments in radio.

"Some night we'll be listening to that fellow talking about the new under-sea radio," chuckled Frank as the talk ceased and the boys laid aside their receivers. "Say, won't it be sport to hear him telling about us and know all the fellows are listening to it?"

"Well, we won't count our chickens just yet," declared Tom sagely. "Just because that receiving set works isn't any proof the sending set will. And without being able to talk back a diver isn't any better off—or at least much better off—if he can hear what's going on in the air."

But Tom might have been far more confident, for the following day when the test was made it worked much better than their most sanguine expectations had led them to think possible. To be sure, their experiments came to an abrupt ending right in the midst of the test, for the sending set on Tom's suit leaked and, with a feeble buzz and sputter, his words trailed off to nothingness.

But when, upon reaching the surface, Rawlins reported that he had heard everything Tom had said and Frank and Henry in the shop had also heard him, the boys knew that their plans and the principles of the outfit were all right and that only the question of making the set absolutely watertight remained to be solved.

"I don't see why it should not be inside the suit," declared Rawlins, as the boys were discussing the matter and were at a loss to know how to accomplish their aims. "You say these wireless waves go through everything and we get them through the suit in the receiving set so why shouldn't they go out through everything just as well. Look here, I was thinking over this last night and here's my idea."

As the boys gathered about, the diver rapidly sketched his plan of a new suit in which the sending set could be placed within a receptacle full of compressed air.

"I believe that *would* work," cried Tom when he grasped Rawlins' scheme. "I don't see why compressed air should affect the outfit any and it's easy enough to make watertight fittings where the wires come out and there's no tuning to do, We can always use a special wave length and if several men were talking under water each one could have his own wave length. Yes. I'll bet you've solved the puzzle, Mr. Rawlins."

Keen on the new plan the boys started a new set, or rather two new sets, for they wished to make a test to determine if two men under water could converse, while Rawlins busied himself on the special suits and air pockets to be used.

"We'll have to balance the weight of the set against the increased buoyancy of this compressed air," he remarked as he worked. "But I see where that's an advantage. One of your troubles has been the weight of batteries and by this air caisson arrangement weight won't cut any figure under water."

"But suppose the air pocket springs a leak?" queried Frank. "We'd be just as badly off as before."

"Well, I don't calculate to have it leak," replied Rawlins, "but if you make the sets as near watertight as you can, they'd still go on working for some time before they got soaked. And if I can't make a little caisson that'll hold a hundred pounds of air for ten or twelve hours I'll give up diving and drive a taxi."

Several days, however, were required to get the set and the air pocket suits ready and when, after a test in the workshop, everything seemed in perfect working order, Tom and Rawlins donned their suits and prepared to descend the ladder through the trapdoor.

Just before his head dipped beneath the surface of the water Tom spoke into his mouthpiece and Frank, listening at his instruments, gave a start as his chum's voice came clearly to his ears.

"So long, old man," came Tom's cheery voice, which somehow Frank had expected would sound muffled. "Keep your ear glued to the set and be ready for great news. I'll bet we give you a surprise."

The next instant only a few bubbles marked the spot where Tom had sunk beneath the surface of the water, and little did he or the others dream how much truth was in his parting words or what an amazing surprise was awaiting not only Frank but himself.

CHAPTER VI—THE RED MENACE

During the weeks while Tom and his friends were busy at their work on the under-sea radio, grave and sinister events were taking place, of which the boys knew little or nothing, but which kept Mr. Pauling, Mr. Henderson and their men in a perpetual state of worry, and of sleepless nights and unceasing work.

Close upon the heels of the unprecedented influx of contraband liquor, which despite every effort continued undiminished and which had completely baffled the officials, came a flood of Bolshevist propaganda of the most dangerous and revolutionary character. Suddenly, and without warning, it had appeared throughout the country. Every town, city and village was filled with it and so cleverly were the circulars, booklets and handbills worded, so logical were the arguments and statements they contained, so appealing to the uneducated foreign element and the dissatisfied army of the unemployed that they were greedily read, accepted and absorbed until the country was menaced by a red revolution and officials went to bed never knowing what bloodshed and destruction the morrow might hold in store.

Almost coincident with this came a wave of crime. Hold-ups, burglars, murders, kidnaping and incendiarism swept like an epidemic through the big cities. Scarcely a day passed that the daily papers did not bear glaring headlines announcing some new and daring crime. Bank messengers, paymasters, cashiers and business men were held up at the point of revolvers or were blackjacked on the public streets in broad daylight. Stores and shops were boldly entered by masked bandits who held up and robbed the clerks and customers alike. Taxis and motor cars were attacked, their occupants beaten into unconsciousness and robbed and the vehicles stolen under the noses of the police. Homes of the rich, banks and business houses were entered and ransacked despite electric burglar alarms and armed guards. Each day the daring criminals grew bolder. From thugs they were changing into murderous bandits; where formerly a man was knocked down or blackjacked the victims were now shot in cold blood. Murders and homicides were of daily occurrence. Even on crowded thoroughfares within sight of hundreds of passers-by men were killed and the bandits escaped and no one felt that life and property were safe. The police seemed powerless and at a loss. Now and then a bandit was captured. Occasionally one would be shot down, wounded or killed by an officer or by some prospective victim, but still the crimes continued unabated. Indeed, the more the police strove to check the bandits the more they appeared to thrive and increase and the bolder they became. Lawlessness was rampant and, while the public wondered, criticized, clamored for protection, and countless theories were put forth, those in the inner circle, the secret agents of the government and the trusted ones, knew that, back of it all, the underlying cause and the root of the evil was the red propaganda which they were powerless to check.

Many were the secret meetings, the closely guarded conferences held between the untiring officers detailed to run the menace to earth, to stamp the venomous Bolshevist serpent underfoot, to bring the country to its safe and sane law-abiding state of the past. And prominent in all such closely guarded, mysterious councils were Mr. Pauling and Mr. Henderson.

"There is some one mind directing it all, in my opinion," declared Mr. Pauling. "Some arch criminal—a Bolshevist emissary—some man with a tremendous brain, marvelous executive ability, immense personal magnetism, but whose mind, heart and soul are warped and twisted. One who is such a criminal as the world has fortunately never known before. If we can lay our hands on him the rest will be easy. Without a leader, without a directive brain, these common criminals will be lost. They are arrant cowards, mere tools and yet, by some almost superhuman power, are controlled, directed, moved like pawns on a chessboard, by an unseen, mysterious being who so far has completely baffled us."

"I agree with you perfectly," said Mr. Henderson. "I believe the same man, the same arch fiend, is back of the rum-running; that this is merely a tryout, a test, to see if we can detect him and that through it all is a deep-laid, dastardly plot to inflame the people and at the same time enrich himself. To my mind, it savors of some one far greater in brain power, in intrigue and in ability than those unshaven, misguided Russians. It looks far more as if it were German work—perhaps some high officer of the Prussian army or navy—who, afraid of his own republican countrymen and filled with a fiendish desire for revenge, is devoting himself to the destruction of law and order in the United States."

"That is very plausible as a theory," remarked another man,

"but it does not get us anywhere. If this is so, where does this master mind stay? Where are his headquarters? Surely he must have underlings,—lieutenants and trusted emissaries and some place, some headquarters, from which his nefarious schemes are sent forth. Nothing comes in by mail or by passengers we know. Every alien who enters is known. Not a word that tends to bear out your theories had been wrung from the men captured even though they were on the verge of death or were about to go to the electric chair. No, I do not agree with you. It's merely the aftermath of the war. Men were taught to handle firearms and to kill their fellow men. They were fed up, encouraged and lived with excitement and constant peril. The war ended; they were out of work, they pined for the thrill of danger and their viewpoint of life, of property and of right and wrong was distorted. Banditry offered an easy way of securing funds; it filled their desire for excitement; it satisfied their grudge against society and their country and, like all crimes which succeed, it became contagious and got a grip on more and more men. It's all the logical outcome of the war and in my opinion the red propaganda has nothing whatever to do with it."

Mr. Henderson smiled. "Perhaps I may be able to change your views, Selwin," he remarked. "I wanted to know your ideas before I came out with it. As you all know, I was on special work during the war—detailed to decode all suspicious messages that came in by radio or cable and to use my vivid imagination to try to find hidden meanings in apparently innocent messages. You all know the result, and there is no need of recalling specific cases, such as the famous sugar shipment to Garcia and the announcement of a baby's birth but which, thanks to my 'hunch' or imagination or whatever you wish to call it, led to the apprehension of the most dangerous female spy of the time and the confiscation of those incriminating documents which saved the *Leviathan* from destruction, prevented several thousand of our boys from going to the bottom of the sea, kept Brooklyn bridge from being blown to bits, thus blocking the Navy Yard, and prevented countless women and children from being widows and orphans. But perhaps you do not all know that, back of that stupendous plot, that greatest attempted coup of the enemy to terrorize and cripple the United States, that supreme effort of a dying, beaten nation to turn the tide of war and transform her from the vanquished to the victor, was the work of one man. To him was entrusted this almost superhuman task. The reward, if he succeeded, was to be honors and riches beyond conception. Had he won he would to-day be seated upon the throne of England—the despotic, iron-handed governor of a German colony with his feet upon the neck of the British people and with the colossal indemnity, which it had been planned to exact from our country, as his monetary reward. If he failed, his life was to pay the forfeit. Not only his life was to be sacrificed, but his lands and property were to be confiscated, his family imprisoned, degraded and exiled. It was, I think, the greatest, the most stupendous gamble ever known. And the gambler lost! By the merest chance, by pure accident, by a coincidence which no human being could have foreseen, his messages—the vital message—came into my hands and, through a tiny mistake, an error which might have passed a thousand eyes unnoticed, the conspirator—this gambler in nations and life—was betrayed and all his efforts, his widespread plots, his carefully organized plans came to nothing. But yet he escaped. Evidently he considered a gambling debt one that could be disregarded. His country, or rather his emperor, had overlooked a most important matter. He had failed to provide for getting hold of the gambler to collect his debt. No doubt, had Germany been victorious, some emissary of the Kaiser would eventually have found this man and would have exacted payment in full. But with Germany's downfall he was safe—at least as long as he remained out of Germany—and so completely did he efface himself that we came to the conclusion that he had committed suicide. But, gentlemen, I am willing to wager my reputation that he still lives. I have evidence which to my mind is absolutely conclusive that he is at the bottom of this Bolshevist propaganda, this influx of liquor, this wave of crime."

Amazed, the others gazed at Mr. Henderson as he paused after this surprising announcement.

"Jove! That's some statement!" cried one. "If you're right, Henderson, we've got our work cut out for us. I can see why he might do it though. I know who you mean—there's no use mentioning names even here. And if it is he I can understand why he has picked on Uncle Sam. But, by Jove, old man, if 'tis he, then watch your step! He's no man to forgive or forget. He'll have his eye on you and mark you for a come-back, I'll wager."

Henderson smiled grimly. "He has already," he remarked dryly. "That's my proof that he's the man. Like all of his kind he's so confoundedly conceited, so cocksure of himself, so puffed up with his own importance that, sooner or later, he's bound to overdo himself. He cannot resist the temptation to let some one know what a big toad in the puddle he is. He must boast or bust and such men always hang themselves if you give them rope enough. Here's the rope he's hung himself with!"

As he finished, Mr. Henderson tossed a sheet of paper on the table and the others crowded close to examine it.

To the casual observer, it would have meant little. A sheet of ordinary note paper with a single line written by a typewriter across it. There was no date, no signature, merely the words: "Remember Mercedes and Garcia." But to these keen-eyed, square-jawed, quiet men those words carried grave import. To them, it meant more than pages of writing might have carried.

"I guess you're right," exclaimed Selwin. "That is, as far as his being alive and this coming from him is concerned. But why do you think he or this has any connection with the other matters?"

"Another coincidence—or perhaps you'll say imagination,"

replied Mr. Henderson. "Examine this pamphlet—the latest effusion of our red propagandists. Do you notice anything peculiar about it?"

Each man shook his head as the flimsy pamphlet passed from hand to hand.

"Very well," commented Mr. Henderson. "You notice that it's not printed—that is, with type. It's a zincotype impression from typewriting. And if you look closely you'll also see that the small "a" has a broken tail, the capital "T" has a little twist in one arm of the top, the small "e" is flattened or battered and the "B" always shows a tiny smudge above it where the character on the same key struck the paper owing to the type bar being bent slightly. Now, kindly examine this terse note I showed you and see if you do not find the identical defects in the same letters."

"By Jove, yes!" cried one, as they again studied the paper. "Henderson, you're a winner. The machine that wrote one wrote the other. Not a shade of a doubt of it. But how about the rest of these dirty sheets and how about the bandits and the liquor?"

"I've examined several thousand circulars and pamphlets," replied Mr. Henderson, "and all that are typewritten are the same. Our friend is doing all the writing on one machine. I imagine he is hanging out somewhere and takes no chances by entrusting his work to outsiders. A man could do all the typing and could make zinc photo plates in a single small room. As for my hunch that the rum-runners are connected with the same gang, it's based on this."

As he spoke, he placed a small metal object on the table, a bit of lead about half an inch in diameter and resembling a small coin. The others picked it up and examined it curiously.

"Well, what's this to do with the matter?" asked one.

"This note," replied Mr. Henderson, "was left at my door and to prevent it from blowing away this bit of lead was placed upon it. You don't see anything suspicious about it, but you may when I draw your attention to the fact that this is a metal seal from a particular brand and make of an extremely high-priced French West Indian liquor. Until the day after I received this reminder of Mercedes and Garcia, there was not, to the best of our knowledge and belief, a single bottle of that Pére Kerrman liqueur in the United States—except possibly in the private stock of some millionaire or exclusive club. Two days later, the country was flooded with it."

"You win!" cried Selwin. "Now about the bandits. Have you got them dead to rights, too?"

"Ask Pauling," replied Mr. Henderson. "He's the next witness."

"Here's my exhibit A," said Mr. Pauling, as he drew a creased paper from an inside pocket and placed it before the assembled officials.

"H-m-m, another threat, eh?" remarked the first one who examined it.

"Yes, commanding me to drop investigation of that hold-up gang that the police nabbed on West 16th St. last week. Nothing was said while the police were at it, but as soon as I took hold I received this."

"And written with the same old machine!" exclaimed Selwin. "All right, Pauling, I may be from Missouri, but you and Henderson have shown me. Now let's plan a campaign."

"If these two notes were sent by the same man, as they appear to have been," remarked a quiet man who heretofore had said nothing but had been steadily consuming one black cigar after another by the process of chewing them between his strong white teeth, "then our game is right underfoot, so to speak— right in little old Manhattan probably."

"Bully for you, Meredith!" cried a small, wiry, nervous man, clapping the other familiarly on the back. "'The mills of the gods,' etc., you know. Where did you fish that idea from?"

"From some place you lack—a brain," retorted Meredith continuing to bite savagely at his cigar. "But, fooling aside," he went on, "it's a cinch he is. Henderson and Pauling get their notes only two days apart and, what's more, Pauling gets his within twenty-four hours after he starts that investigation. No time for word to get any other place and have a bit of type-written paper get back."

"Huh! Then, according to you, all this red rubbish is also written right in the old home-town, eh?" snorted the thin man.

"Yep," replied Meredith. "Expect that's why we haven't nailed its source yet. Fact is, I believe there isn't any rum being smuggled in. Been stored here and just being distributed now. Bet we've all been walking over the trail star-gazing. So darned sure it was all coming in from outside we never thought of it being right alongside of us."

"That's a possibility," admitted Henderson and then, dropping their voices, the half dozen men earnestly discussed plans, offered suggestions, examined mysterious documents stored in a hidden and massive safe in the wall and pored over maps and diagrams which no one, outside of this inner circle, would ever see.

At the end of two hours, the conference broke up. The papers and documents were replaced in their secret vault, the maps and diagrams were locked in a steel box and thrust in another safe and the men chatted on various matters, discussing the latest news, arguing the respective merits of motor cars, expressing opinions as to the next pennant winner, telling jokes and thoroughly enjoying themselves as if they had not a care in the world and were not literally carrying their lives in their hands day and night.

"What's that boy of yours doing in radio now?" asked Meredith, addressing Mr. Pauling when the conversation finally turned towards wireless. "Henderson was telling me about their 'radio detective' stuff. Great kid—Tom."

"Oh, he and Frank Putney are working on a submarine radio scheme. I met a young chap at Nassau with a new-fangled diving suit and he and the boys are trying to work out a radio outfit to use under water. Say, they're succeeding, too."

"Jove! that's a great scheme!" exclaimed another. "Under-sea wireless! Well, I'll be hanged, what won't our kids be up to next!"

"Wish we'd had anything as good to tinker with when we were kids," declared Selwin. "I remember how every one laughed at Marconi when he first started wireless. My boy's crazy over it now. Well, I must be getting on."

Rising, Selwin slipped from the room, sauntered casually about the corridor, noted the seemingly inattentive janitor brushing imaginary dust from a window frame, knew that the lynx-eyed guard was on his job, and without a sign of recognition made his way to the elevator and the street. At intervals of half an hour or so the others left, some by the same corridor, others through an outer room, where an office boy seemed dozing in a chair over a lurid, paper-covered novel—but upon whose boyish, freckled cheeks a closely-shaven, heavy beard might have been detected by a near examination—while still others took a roundabout route and descended to the street on the opposite side of the building. At last, only Mr. Pauling and Henderson were left and the two friends, glad of a chance to have a quiet smoke and to be free from care for a short time, sat chatting and talking over Mr. Pauling's last trip to the West Indies.

"It was positively baffling," stated Mr. Pauling in reply to a question. "I knew they were filled to the gunwales with liquor and I knew as well as I wanted to that the cargo was going to the States and yet, when they got here and our men boarded them they were either empty or carried legitimate cargoes or else they never touched our ports and came back empty. It's common talk that the stuff is going to us, but no one has given away how it's done yet. Why, I even had one trailed—shadowed by a disguised cutter—and they kept her within sight for days and then I'll be hanged if she didn't come back without a sign of cargo. Now where did they land it? Only solution is they got cold feet and heaved it overboard."

"More likely they met some other craft during the night and transhipped," suggested Mr. Henderson. "I imagine that's how they get it in. Have some prearranged signal and spot and ship the stuff in at another port while they sail boldly into harbor. Of course we're watching for them and let up on other places and while we're boarding the suspect the other craft gets in on some unfrequented bit of coast and meets a truck or car. It's not hard. We can't guard *all* the coast with our force and I'm sure that game's played sometimes, if not always. We've taken a lot of stuff that afterwards proved to be colored water or cane-juice and of course they didn't bring that from Cuba or the Bahamas just for the sake of getting our goats."

"And then there were the Chinese," resumed Mr. Pauling. "Of course there we've another difficulty because, once set ashore or near shore, John can look after himself and doesn't need a truck to carry him out of our sight. Just the same I'd give a lot to know the secret of their putting it over on us."

"I've often wondered if those boys—Tom and Frank— weren't right about that strange conversation they overheard," ruminated Mr. Henderson. "I'm morally certain they were all right in their cross bearings with their loops, although I didn't tell them so—and yet we found nothing there. Have you asked the boys if they've heard anything more of it lately?"

"No, but I will," Mr. Pauling replied. "They've been so busy with this new idea I expect they've forgotten all about it. I promised I'd go down to see their— Hello, there's the phone. Wonder who 'tis."

Leaning forward, Mr. Pauling drew the extension phone towards him, lifted the receiver and placed it at his ear.

"Yes, this is Mr. Pauling speaking," he said. Then his face blanched, his cigar dropped from his fingers and in anxious, frightened tones he cried, "What's that you say? Frank! What's that? Tom under water! Calling for help! Having a fight with—with what? Never mind! Calling through the radio! Yes, I'll be down instantly!"

Slamming the receiver on its hook Mr. Pauling leaped to his feet.

"It's Frank!" he cried. "Says Tom's calling for help from under water. Lord knows what's up! Send Jameson and a bunch of men. Order a patrol down. Rawlins' dock, foot of 28th. You know the place. Come yourself, too!"

Jerking open a drawer, Mr. Pauling grabbed up a heavy revolver, shoved it into his pocket, dashed through the door and as he passed the supposed janitor gave a terse order. "Get inside!" he exclaimed, "Henderson needs you." The next instant he was plunging down the stairs. With a bound he cleared the last few steps, hurtled like a football player through the pedestrians on the sidewalk, leaped into his waiting car and the next instant was violating every traffic law as he drove madly through the streets. Once only did he slacken speed when, as he rounded the corner, he caught a glimpse of one of his men and with a gesture summoned him. Instantly, the man obeyed, leaped on the running board and as the machine again darted ahead clambered in beside Mr. Pauling.

Before Mr. Pauling's footsteps had sounded on the stairs, before the secret service man in the janitor's overalls could dodge inside the room, Mr. Henderson was talking over a private wire to the nearest police station. Ten seconds later, he was rushing downstairs with the erstwhile janitor at his heels and hard on the wake of Mr. Pauling's car his runabout went tearing in the same direction.

As they swung from Fourth Avenue into 28th St., gaping crowds lined the sidewalks craning their necks and peering down the street where, far ahead, the police patrol was startling the neighborhood with its clanging bell as it followed the lead of Mr. Pauling's car.

What had happened, what danger was menacing his boy, Mr. Pauling could not guess. But that Tom was in deadly peril he felt sure. Frank's agonized tones proved that, and while his incoherent, stammering words carried no explanation Mr. Pauling knew that his son was calling for aid from under the water, that something terrible had occurred. Through his mind had instantly flashed the threat of the bandit chief, the threat to make him sweat blood if he continued his investigations. Could it be that? Had the thugs captured or attacked Tom to injure his father? And where was Rawlins? With nerves already strained from overwork and failure to accomplish what the government demanded of him, Mr. Pauling, who was noted for his self-possession, his calmness and clear-headedness in the most trying and perilous moments, was now mad with fear and his teeth actually chattered with nervousness. His car, racing at break-neck speed, seemed almost to crawl. Every corner seemed to be purposely blocked by traffic. He thought he had never seen so many persons crossing the streets, so many slow-moving, horse-drawn vehicles impeding his progress. He cursed aloud, handled his levers with savage jerks, gritted his teeth and mentally prayed he would not be too late. Now, behind him, he could hear the clanging, oncoming patrol truck—he knew Henderson had lost no time. Before him lay the end of the street, the river and the docks. With a reckless twist he swung the car into the waterfront street, took the turn on two wheels, drove it diagonally, regardless of cursing truck-men, across the cobbled road, and with squealing brakes, brought it to a skidding stop by Rawlins' dock. Before it had lost headway he had leaped out, the detective at his side, and as he burst into the boys' work-shop a crowd of blue-clad policemen were jumping from the still moving patrol and were crowding at his heels.

CHAPTER VII—THE CRY FROM

THE DEPTHS

Henry watched Tom's head disappear, he saw the little silvery bubbles rising, for an instant he could distinguish the darker shadow in the water which marked his friend, and then nothing but the rippling green surface of the river was visible through the open trapdoor in the floor of the dock. He and Frank were alone, Tom and Rawlins were beneath the river, and yet, down there at the bottom of the gurgling water, the unseen two could hear every word spoken in the room above. It was marvelous, fantastic and almost incredible. But even more wonderful and impossible events were about to take place. Frank had already heard Tom's parting words over the set, although not a sound had issued from his helmet, and now, with the others under the water, Frank was again talking.

"Yes, I can hear you finely," he said. "Say, it's wonderful. Where are you? Right under the dock? I'm going to let Henry talk to you. I feel as if I were dreaming!"

As Henry listened at the set and Tom's words came to his ears he actually jumped, for he had never expected the words to come as plainly and distinctly as if Tom had been in the room with him and talking to him direct.

"That you, Henry?" came Tom's voice. "Gee, but it's great. I can hear you just as well as if I were up there. Does my voice sound loud?"

"Loud as if you were standing alongside of me," Henry assured him. "I can't believe you're really under water."

So, for some time, the three boys and Rawlins conversed, chatting and laughing, expressing their wonder and delight in boyish expletives and overjoyed at finding their plans and their work had proved such an immense success.

"We're going off a ways," announced Tom, at last. "Mr. Rawlins wants to find out how far away we can hear and send. We're going to walk down the river. You keep talking and after we've gone a few hundred yards we'll call you. If you don't reply that you heard us we'll keep walking back and trying until you do get us. Then we'll know our range."

For a time, the two boys on the dock kept up a steady conversation with Tom and Rawlins, and, much to their surprise, the sounds of their friends' voices continued as loud as when they were directly under the dock.

"It's a funny thing," remarked Frank during a lull in the under-sea conversation, "I thought they'd get out of range very soon. I never would have believed that these little fifty-meter waves could carry that far with only a two-foot grid for an aërial. The water must be a heap better for waves than the air."

Then there was an interval when no sounds came in and Frank was about to call to Tom when, to his ears, came a suppressed "Wha—wha" followed by a hoarse "Sssh!"

Whether Rawlins had intended this for Tom or himself Frank did not know, but he decided that, for some unknown reason, the diver wished silence and so wisely refrained from speaking.

"I would like to know what Mr. Rawlins wanted to be quiet for," said Frank, holding his hand over the mouthpiece of his microphone. "But I suppose there's some good reason for it."

Scarcely had he ceased speaking when he was startled by a sharp exclamation of surprise from Tom.

So unexpected was it that Frank responded involuntarily. "What's that you said?" he asked, exactly as though Tom had been there in the room. But there was no audible reply, merely some faint sounds like subdued whispers, followed by silence.

"Gee, there's something mighty funny going on!" exclaimed Frank, addressing Henry. "Tom said 'Gosh' something and then, when I answer he doesn't say a thing—just some little sounds like whispers. Say, I *do* wonder what they're up to!"

"Oh, I expect they're trying to see if they can talk together without your hearing them," suggested Henry. "Probably that's why Mr. Rawlins told you to be quiet."

"Well, I'm going to find out," declared Frank. "They've no

right to keep us wondering like this."

"Hello!" he cried into the microphone. "What on earth's the matter? I haven't heard a word from you two for five minutes. Can you hear me?"

But instead of Tom's voice in reply Frank was amazed to hear thick, guttural words rapidly spoken, and among them he made out only one that he understood, the name "Oleander."

"Henry!" exclaimed Frank, speaking in hushed tones as if he feared being overheard, "Henry, there's that fellow talking again—the one you and Mr. Rawlins heard—talking in Dutch or something!"

Then the strange voices ceased and very faintly and indistinctly Frank heard Tom's voice asking,

"What does it mean?"

Frank was puzzled. "What does what mean?" he inquired into the microphone. But the reply, if Tom made one, was drowned out and confused by Rawlins' voice. Frank could not distinguish all the words, but he knew from the sounds and intonations that Tom and the diver were discussing some matter between them and he refrained from interrupting.

Then the voices ceased and Frank called, begging Tom to explain matters, asking if anything was wrong. But for a moment there was no reply and he wondered if his voice could be heard.

Then to his ears came Tom's familiar "Gosh!" a few unintelligible words and a shrill whistle, followed by Rawlins' voice. Part of it Frank could not catch but as he strained his ears he distinctly heard Rawlins exclaim:

"We're in a dangerous place! Come on. Let me go first!"

Frank's face paled. "Jehoshaphat!" he exclaimed to Henry who, realizing that something mysterious was taking place beneath the river, was bending close. "Jehoshaphat! They're in danger! Say, what *can* it be? Maybe they're caught in quicksand or a current or under a boat."

Pleadingly, with fright and worry expressed in his tones,

Frank begged Tom to reply, to tell him what was wrong, what the danger was. For a space he waited anxiously for his chum's reply and then, at last, it came.

"It's all right," called Tom. "Don't worry. Stop talking and just listen!"

Frank turned to Henry and disconnected the microphone by throwing off a switch to make sure that no sound could be sent.

"I guess they're all right," he said. "But I'm worried just the same. Why should he want me to be quiet and just listen. Oh, I *do* wish they'd come back."

"There's those foreign words again," he announced presently, "and, say—I didn't think of it before—there are two talking now."

Then followed silence, not a sound, not even a hum or buzz of interference greeted his ears and anxiously he listened, half fearful that some awful casualty had happened to Tom and Rawlins out there somewhere under the turbid waters of the river.

The moments passed terribly slowly to the two boys and then Frank again gave a start as he heard Tom ejaculate "Gosh!" followed by some rapid low-spoken words, only one of which Frank could catch—the word "wreck."

"That's it," he announced to Henry with a sigh of relief. "They've found a wreck. Gee! perhaps they've found treasure."

Henry laughed gayly. "Oh, that's good!" he exclaimed. "Treasure in the East River! You must think you're down in the West Indies or somewhere."

"Well, I don't see what's so awful funny about finding a wreck or treasure in the East River," declared Frank petulantly. "Lots of boats have sunk here and why shouldn't one of 'em have treasure on it? I don't mean millions of dollars worth of gold or jewels of course—like pirates' treasure—but there might be a box of money or something."

"You're way off," replied Henry. "They wouldn't leave a

wreck here for a week. They'd get it up or blow it up right away. Why, a wreck here would block the channel. No, sir, you heard 'em wrong."

"I did not!" stoutly maintained Frank. "I know Tom said something about a wreck. I don't care what you say. How do you know there isn't some old wreck out there somewhere? It may have been there for years; how would any one know?"

"Why, Mr. Rawlins and Tom aren't the only divers who ever went down here," insisted Henry. "The city and the government and wrecking companies and contractors have divers going down all the time. I've watched 'em working heaps of times. Father's a construction engineer and I know he always has divers at work around New York. Some of 'em would have found a wreck if it had been there."

"Well, anyway we'll know pretty soon," said Frank. "They can't stay down much longer. They must—"

With a startled cry his words ended and his scared, pale face told Henry that something dreadful had happened. Ringing in Frank's ears, shrill, filled with deadly terror, the shriek of a boy frightened almost out of his senses, came Tom's despairing cry—a wordless, awful scream.

"What's the matter?" Frank forced his paralyzed tongue to form the words. "Tom! Oh, Tom! What's wrong? Why did you yell?"

"Help! Send for help!" rang back the answer. "It's awful"— followed by words so filled with mortal terror that Frank could make nothing of them and then—"Get Dad! Get the police!"

Frank waited to hear no more. Dropping the receivers he leaped across the room, jerked the receiver from the telephone and frantically called for Mr. Pauling's number. But in his fright and terror, his fear for Tom, his hurried words were a mere jumble to the operator.

"Can't hear you," came the girl's voice. "What number did you say?"

Again Frank yelled. "Watkins 6636!" he cried, striving to make his words clear.

"Watkins 3666?" inquired the girl, and Frank could almost hear her masticating gum.

"No, 6636!" he screamed. "Hurry!"

The seconds that followed seemed like years to Frank. Across his brain flashed a thousand fears and he suffered untold agonies as he stood there, sweat pouring from his face. What if Mr. Pauling should not be in his office? Suppose the line were busy? What if the girl got the wrong number? How slow she was! Had she forgotten the call? Would no one answer? And then, when he was sure he must have waited hours, his heart gave a great leap, a load seemed lifted from his mind as he heard Mr. Pauling's cheery, deep-throated:

"Hello! Who is it?"

"It's Frank!" fairly screamed the boy. "Tom's in trouble! I don't know what—he's under the river—with Mr. Rawlins. He wants help! Sent for you! Wants police!"

Then, when at last Mr. Pauling had succeeded in grasping the message and in excited tones had shouted, "All right, I'll be down instantly!" Frank sank limply to the floor.

But the next second he was up and at the table by the radio set.

"Have you heard anything?" he inquired anxiously of Henry, who had taken up the receivers and had been listening while Frank called Mr. Pauling.

"Not a word," replied Henry.

"Oh, gosh! Oh, I *do* wish they'd hurry!" exclaimed Frank. "Oh, they're terribly slow! And how *will* they get to him? How do we know where he is?"

Slowly the minutes dragged by. Each tick of the cheap clock on the table seemed to spell Tom's fate and still no sound came from beneath the river. Once, Henry thought he caught a word, an exclamation half suppressed, but he could not be sure. He had called Tom, but no reply had come. Were the two dead? Had some awful calamity overtaken them at the bottom of the river? Was this to be the tragic end of all their experiments? Was Tom's death the reward for their success?

Then, from far up the street, came the clamor of a bell, and the screech of a motor horn sounded from nearer at hand.

At the same instant Henry uttered a glad, joyous cry. "They're all right!" he shouted. "I just heard Rawlins tell Tom to go ahead!"

With a quick motion, he threw in the switch and at that moment Frank's ringing shout of joy filled the room.

But before Henry could call to Tom, before he could utter a sound, hurrying, tramping footsteps echoed from the dock, the door burst inwards with a bang and into the room leaped Mr. Pauling. Beside him was a heavy-jawed man with drawn pistol and over his shoulder through the open doorway the boys saw the visored caps and blue coats of police.

"They're safe!" yelled Frank, trying to make his voice heard above the excited, shouted interrogations of Mr. Pauling. "We just heard them."

Mr. Pauling leaped towards the open trapdoor, the police crowding at his heels. Henry dropped his instruments and joined them and all crowded forward.

A shadow seemed to hover in the dull water and a slender affair of wire broke the surface.

"They're here!" screamed Frank.

"Thank God!" echoed Mr. Pauling fervently.

Hardly had the words of thankfulness left his lips when he uttered a startled cry, and, throwing himself face downward at the edge of the trapdoor, plunged his arms into the swirling water. The dim shadowy form of the diver whose helmet had just appeared, had swayed to one side; his hands, clutching the upper rungs of the ladder, had loosened their grasp, his arms had wavered and had taken a feeble stroke as if trying to swim and from the receiver on the table had issued a despairing cry, a choking, gurgling groan, ending in a gasp.

Whether the swaying, half-floating form was Tom or Rawlins, Mr. Pauling could not know, for in the suits identity was lost, but trained as he was through long years in a service where to act instinctively meant life or death, he instantly dropped to the floor and clutched at the dim figure beneath. Had he delayed for the fraction of a second he would have been too late, but, as it was, his fingers closed on one of the diver's wrists. The next instant he had grasped the other arm and a moment later, with Henderson's aid, he had dragged the dripping, limp form onto the dock and the two men were cutting the suit and helmet from the unconscious form. But they already knew it was Tom. The boy's limbs projecting from the short tunic had proved this and Mr. Pauling's face was white and strained as they dragged the khaki-colored garment and the helmet from his son.

"Thank Heaven Rawlins fixed those suits so he could not breathe flames!" exclaimed Mr. Henderson, as the helmet was drawn from Tom's head. "He's breathing, Pauling!"

As he spoke, there was a disturbance at the door and the police stood aside as an ambulance surgeon pushed his way hurriedly into the room. He bent over Tom in silence for an instant and then he glanced up and Mr. Pauling read good news in his eyes.

"Don't worry!" he exclaimed. "He's not hurt. Hasn't breathed any water. Just in a faint, I think. He'll be around in a moment. Hello! Here's another!"

While he had been speaking, another helmeted form had appeared, dragging a limp figure, and, holding to the latter's legs still another diver was climbing up the ladder.

"What the dickens!" exclaimed Mr. Henderson glancing up. "Who the devil are these? Two divers go down and four come up!"

Dropping the apparently lifeless diver on the floor Rawlins

dragged off his helmet, glanced about in a puzzled way and then, without waiting to ask questions exclaimed, "Here, Doctor! Quick! Get at this chap!"

At his words, the doctor and his assistant sprang to the side of the form on the floor and rapidly stripped off his helmet and, as the man's face was exposed, even the hardened surgeons could not restrain a gasp of horror and amazement. The face was horrible to look upon. It was scorched, seared, blackened, the eyebrows burned off, the eyelids hanging in shreds, the sight-less eyes staring white and opaque like those of a boiled fish. Rawlins gave a single glance at him.

"Oh, Lord!" he ejaculated. "He's done for! He's had flames from the chemicals in his helmet! Poor devil, he *must* have suffered!"

Then, turning to Mr. Henderson, he exclaimed.

"Better get the suit off this other chap. Don't know who he is, but he's something rotten! Guess it's a good thing the police are here."

As Mr. Henderson and Rawlins stepped towards the man who still wore his suit, the fellow raised an arm and leaped, or tried to leap, away, quite forgetting the heavy, lead-soled boots he wore. The result was that he tripped and fell heavily and, before Rawlins or Henderson could reach him, he was twisting and rolling towards the gaping trapdoor. An instant more and he would have been in the water, but just as he reached the edge of the opening, Frank, who with Henry had been staring open-mouthed and dumbfounded at the surprising and incom-prehensible events taking place so rapidly before them, sprang forward and slammed shut the door which, in falling, pinned the fellow's legs beneath it. Then, as if fearing the man might wriggle free, the excited boy jumped upon the heavy planks. But there was no fight or attempt to escape left in the fellow and, as several policemen rushed forward and seized him, he submitted without the least resistance and a moment later had been stripped of his suit.

Once more it was Mr. Henderson's turn to be amazed, for, as he caught sight of the man's face, as he saw the closely-cropped, bullet-shaped head, the tiny, close-set piggish eyes and the big loose-lipped mouth he could scarcely believe his eyes and uttered a sharp exclamation of wonder.

"Put the bracelets on him and don't give him a chance!" he ordered the police and, as the shining irons snapped with a click about the man's wrists and the officers led him to one side, the small piglike eyes glared at Mr. Henderson with such mingled hatred, brutality and ferocity that the boys shivered.

Rawlins was now bending above Tom beside Mr. Pauling and when, a moment later, the boy took a long, deep breath and his eyes fluttered open, the anxious, strained expression upon the diver's face vanished.

"I'll say he's a good sport!" he ejaculated. "Poor kid! Don't wonder he went clean off! And he saved my life too—with his under-sea radio at that!"

CHAPTER VIII—ASTOUNDING DISCOVERIES

Perhaps it may seem as if the boys had met with success too easily and had accomplished far more in a short time than would be possible. But as a matter of fact they had encountered innumerable difficulties, had made numbers of mistakes, had been faced with failure or negative results time after time and would have given up in despair had it not been for the encouragement of Mr. Pauling and Mr. Henderson and the never-ceasing optimism of Rawlins. Indeed, Rawlins had done fully as much to make the under-sea radio a success as had the boys.

Although he did not or could not become an adept at radio and insisted that it was all Greek to him, yet he was a born inventor and a mechanical genius. He had been diving since he was a mere boy, his father and grandfather had made deep-sea diving their profession, and he felt as much at home under water as on land. Hence, to him, there was nothing mysterious or baffling about the depths and he could see no valid reason why anything that could be accomplished on shore should not be accomplished equally well under water. He had distinguished himself by devising a submarine apparatus for taking motion pictures at the bottom of the sea and it was while engaged in making a sub-sea film that he had invented and perfected his remarkable self-contained diving suit. To him, with his experience, the shortcomings of the suit—the danger of the chemicals flaming up if they came in contact with water—were of no moment, for, as he had explained to the boys, he automatically shut the valve if for any reason he removed his lips from the breathing tube, the action being as natural and unconscious as holding one's breath when swimming under water.

But he at once realized that if the suits were to become a commercial or practical thing, or if the under-sea radio was to be used, it would be necessary to make the apparatus absolutely safe and fool proof. He therefore set to work at once to devise an entirely new system and absolutely refused to allow the boys to don suits and go down until he had thoroughly tested out and proved the new equipment. It was not an easy matter, but in the end he succeeded, and, risking his own life in the experiment, he gave the safety suit a most severe tryout. It fulfilled his greatest expectations and feeling sure that no matter how careless or inexperienced the wearer might be there could be no accident, as far as the suit and oxygen generator were concerned, he was satisfied.

He freely expressed his satisfaction and his indebtedness to the boys, insisting that if it had not been for them and their radio he never would have improved the suit and made it practical for any one to use without danger. In addition, there were innumerable other changes and alterations which had to be made to adapt the suits to radio work, and so, by the time the boys were ready to make their tests, they were using suits which bore but little resemblance to those Rawlins had first shown them.

Upon the helmets were the odd grids of wire at right angles like some great crown; the compressed air receptacles containing the sending sets were attached to the shoulders like old-fashioned knapsacks, and the front of the helmet resembled some grotesque monster's head with the protuberance which contained the compact little receiving set like a huge goiter. Indeed, as Henry had remarked when he first saw Rawlins appearing dripping from the river, they looked like weird and fearful sea monsters. So, if the reader imagines that the boys and Rawlins had had an easy time or that their success was of the phenomenal kind which occurs only in fiction, he is greatly mistaken and the impression is due wholly to the fact that their failures and troubles have not been chronicled.

And now, having explained this, let us return to the boys when, their sub-sea sending set complete, the test was about to take place. As Tom sank beneath the water and slowly descended the ladder he was more excited and thrilled than ever before, for he was about to try an experiment which, if successful, would mark a new era in radio telephony and he was keyed up to a high pitch when at last he dropped from the final rung of the ladder and settled, half-floating like some big, ungainly fish upon the river bottom. Through the half opaque green water he could see the irregular, grotesquely distorted and hazy form of Rawlins appearing gigantic and phantomlike. He might have been fifteen or fifty feet away, for despite the fact that Tom had been down several times he could never accustom himself to the deceptive effects of distance under water and when he stretched his hand towards the indistinct figure he gave an involuntary start when he found Rawlins within arm's length. As his hand touched the clammy rubber surface he uttered an exclamation of surprise and the next instant gave a joyful yell, for at his ejaculation he had heard Rawlins' voice in his ears asking, "What's wrong?"

"For heaven's sake, don't yell so!" came Rawlins' words in

response to Tom's, "Hurrah, it's working!"

"I'll tell the world it's working!" continued the diver, "but don't shout. I'm talking in my lowest tones. Here, how do you like this?"

Tom's ears were almost split as a thunderous bellow filled his helmet, and involuntarily he clapped his hands to the outside of his helmet over his ears.

"That's a lesson," he said in his lowest tones. "Sorry I didn't know, Mr. Rawlins. It won't happen again. I guess these helmets act like sounding boards or something. Hello, there's Frank's voice."

Clear and distinct they could hear Frank asking if there was trouble and Tom barely checked another outburst as he realized that the boys on shore could talk with them and could hear what was going on under the water.

"We can hear everything you say," went on Frank's voice. "Can you hear us and each other?"

"Gee, you bet we can!" replied Tom. "Isn't this just great?"

"Say, are you whispering?" inquired Frank. "I can hardly hear your voice."

"No, but don't shout so," answered Tom. "Down here everything just roars. We have to talk low or we'll deafen each other. I'll bet we don't need head phones on our ears under water."

"Henry's going to talk with you," Frank announced, "he's just crazy to try."

For the next half hour the boys talked back and forth between the workshop and the bottom of the river and then Rawlins and Tom ascended the ladder and removed their suits.

For fully five minutes, the boys pranced, danced, hurrahed, yelled, laughed and made such a racket celebrating their success that it was a wonder the river police did not break in thinking a horde of Indians had taken possession of the dock. And if the truth must be told, Rawlins was just about as excited and acted as crazily as the youngsters.

But at last they calmed down and Frank, mad to go down, donned Tom's suit.

"Try it without the phones," Tom advised him. "Then you can talk loudly enough to be heard up here without deafening Mr. Rawlins."

To Tom, listening at the set on the dock, it seemed little short of uncanny to hear Rawlins and Frank talking from under the water, and indeed, it impressed him as even more remarkable than hearing those on shore when he was below the surface.

Both Rawlins and Frank assured him that the sets worked far better without the receivers on their heads, and even when Frank spoke in his loudest tones Rawlins replied that it did not deafen him as before.

"Now let's try tuning, Frank," said Tom. "I'm going to vary my wave length and see if you can pick it up. Then change yours and I'll see if I can get you."

As Tom spoke, he altered the sending waves slightly and breathlessly waited. Presently Frank's voice came in.

"Got it!" he exclaimed. "Had a bit of trouble at first, but it's all right now. Now see if you can get this."

As he spoke his words ended in a high, shrill squeal, but an instant later, as Tom turned the knob on his tuner, the words suddenly returned in a most startling way, the squeal seeming to change magically into words.

"Hurrah, I got it!" cried Tom jubilantly. "Come on up, Frank, Henry wants a chance."

"You've certainly struck a wonderful thing here," declared Rawlins, when he and Henry came up and had removed their suits. "How far do you suppose it will work?"

"That's something we'll have to find out," replied Tom. "But the sounds come so loudly I'll bet it's good for a long distance. Somehow or other we get sound a lot louder inside a helmet than outside. I don't just get the reason, but I expect it's either because the whole air vibrates to the diaphragm of the receivers inside the helmet and no sound waves are lost or else because the helmet itself acts like a sounding board or maybe there are some sort of amplified waves set up."

"I guess it's the air being inclosed," said Rawlins. "When I used to wear a regular suit and used an ordinary phone under water it was the same way, but I never thought of it in connection with radio. The whole thing gets me, there's millions in this if we can patent it. Let's go down once more and give her a real tryout. We'll take a hike down river a few hundred yards and see if the boys get us. If they don't we'll come back and keep trying and if they do we'll go on down as far as we can. Then, if we find it's O. K. we'll try to get your folks to let you go down to Nassau and we'll show the world, I'll bet."

"That's a good idea," agreed Tom. "You keep listening and now and then talking, Frank, and as soon as we lose your voice we'll send and then walk back until we get you again. That way we can find if we can hear farther than you can or whether it's the other way about."

Donning their suits, Tom and Rawlins once more descended the ladder and half-floating, half-walking turned downstream. Rawlins had already cautioned Tom to keep close to his side and to hold to his hand, for, with the mud stirred up by their feet and carried by the current with them, it was impossible to see more than a few feet and Rawlins knew the danger that lay in becoming separated.

Even with the radio connecting them with the boys on the surface Tom might easily get confused and hopelessly lost if he strayed or was carried from sight of Rawlins and while Tom knew that, by turning on more oxygen, he could bob to the surface, yet danger lurked in this as he might emerge in the path of some steamer or motor boat and be run down or torn to pieces with the propellers. As long as they kept close to shore, following the docks and piers, there was no danger, for the only vessels in the vicinity were canal boats and barges which were not in use, the piers for several hundred yards having been used merely for storage and as warehouses for some time. Moreover, by keeping under the docks they were perfectly safe and Rawlins had no intention of going out into the channel with its swift currents and constantly passing tugs, ferryboats and small craft. So, half feeling his way and moving by the diver's intuitive sixth sense of direction and holding to Tom's hand, Rawlins moved slowly down the river.

Frank's words were constantly in their ears and now and then they replied, and somehow to Tom there was a most remarkable sensation of making no progress whatsoever. There was nothing visible by which to gauge their motion and, as the voice through the set continued to sound exactly the same and did not grow fainter with distance, he seemed to be standing still, although exerting himself and constantly stepping or rather pushing himself forward. He was so intent on this and so interested in the novel experience that he scarcely realized that Frank's voice had suddenly grown faint and was interrupted by an odd buzzing sound which instantly brought back the memory of the sounds they had heard when listening to the mysterious speaker with their loop aërials. He was just about to speak and ask Frank if he could hear when he felt Rawlins jerk his arm. He floundered forward and the next instant was dragged between the spiles of a dock where the water was dark with shadows.

"What,—what—" he began, but instantly checked his words as a low "Ssh!" from Rawlins reached his ears. Not knowing what had happened or why Rawlins had suddenly acted in this strange manner, confused and bewildered, Tom peered about through the murky water. At first he saw nothing save the surrounding spiles, seeming to move and sway in dim, shadowy forms—the bottom of a canal boat with yard-long streamers of sea weeds waving from its barnacle-encrusted planks; a piece of trailing, rusty cable; a few rotting, water-soaked timbers protruding from the mud; and a shapeless mass which might have been almost any piece of jetsam cast into the river. Then like phantom shapes, so indistinct, hazy and formless that he was not sure they were not shadows in the water, he saw two figures—two moving things that, for a brief instant, he thought must be huge, dull-green fish nosing about the mud. And then, as he gazed fixedly at them from between the spiles, a strange unreasoning fear clutched at his heart and he felt an odd, prickly sensation on his scalp and at the back of his neck, for the moving, sinister, unnatural things were approaching, moving noiselessly, slowly, but certainly towards him as though they had scented his presence and were bent on hunting him out.

What were they? What strange, unknown, impossible sea monsters were these? He was frightened, shaking, and in his terror had forgotten completely about the radio outfit. Glad, indeed, was Tom that Rawlins was beside him, that the diver was armed—for Rawlins, he knew, never went down without a hatchet in his belt ready for use in case of an emergency such as fouling a rope or timber. But why didn't Rawlins speak? Why had he ordered him to be silent? The sea monsters could not hear; what was the reason?

And then, so suddenly that it came as a shock, he realized that the approaching forms, the grotesque shapes, were no sea creatures, no gigantic savage fish, but men! Men in diving suits much like their own. Men walking in the odd, half-sprawling, half-floating, forward-leaning posture he knew so well. But great as was Tom's relief at this discovery his wonderment was doubly increased. Who were they and what were they doing here? Why had Rawlins drawn him into hiding? What did it all mean? Then, just as he was about to disregard Rawlins' whispered orders and ask, the two figures disappeared. Without reason, without warning, they vanished from sight as if by magic.

So dumbfounded was Tom that involuntarily he uttered an ejaculation of surprise and fairly jumped when, faint but clear, he heard Frank ask, "What's that you said?"

But before he could reply, Rawlins was speaking. "Come on!" he whispered, his voice being as low as if he feared the others might hear and, quite forgetting that he was under water, cut off from all conversation with other human beings save the boys. "Come on, I don't know who they are, but there's something funny. They've got suits like mine and the Lord knows who they are or how they got 'em. I'm going to find out where they went."

Slipping between the spiles with their slimy, weed-grown surfaces, Rawlins, holding to Tom's hand, struggled forward into the lighter water. Beside them rose a dark wall of masonry and reaching this Rawlins proceeded to feel his way along it. Before they had traveled ten feet the diver uttered a sharp ejaculation. Beside them in the wall, loomed a huge, black hole, the mouth of a great sewer.

"They went in here," whispered Rawlins. "Come on!"

A moment later they were in utter blackness, feeling their way forward along the walls.

And now, very thin and faint, Tom heard Frank's voice again. "What on earth's the matter?" he asked. "I haven't heard a word from you two for five minutes. Can you hear me?"

Tom was about to answer for they were evidently at nearly the limit of receiving range and his mouth opened, his lips formed the words of his reply, but no sound issued from them. Clear, loud and harsh, guttural words rang in Tom's ears. This was not Frank's voice nor Henry's; the words were not even English. Amazed and uncomprehending Tom was speechless and then, among the incomprehensible foreign syllables, came a word he recognized, the one word "Oleander!"

Instantly he knew that by some strange freak, by some mystifying coincidence he was again hearing that unknown man to whom he had so often listened. It seemed strange, weird, uncanny to have it coming to his ears here in the old disused sewer, but after all, he reflected, why not? Rawlins had heard it once before, there was nothing remarkable about it and he was on the point of asking his companion if he had heard and of trying to tell Frank, when once more his words were stayed. Before him the stygian darkness suddenly grew light, a brilliant beam stabbed down from overhead and through the strangely illuminated water Tom saw the two men in diving suits standing beneath a square opening down which a ladder was being thrust. But why, he vaguely wondered, was the water so transparent? How was it that he could now see clearly for many yards? And then, with a start, it dawned upon him that he was not looking through water, that there was nothing between him and the trap save air. He was standing with head and shoulders out of water.

And now the gruff, guttural words were once more beating in his ears and the next instant he saw the strange divers seize a dangling rope, tipped with a great iron hook, dip it under the water and then, as the hook again ascended, he saw a dripping, cigar-shaped object like a torpedo slowly rise from the water and disappear in the opening above. Close behind it the two divers followed up the ladder, the ladder was drawn up, the light snapped out and the next instant Tom and Rawlins were once more in absolute darkness.

"What does it all mean?" exclaimed Tom, finding his voice at last.

"What does what—" commenced Frank's voice, only to be overwhelmed and drowned out by Rawlins' louder words.

"Search me!" replied the latter. "Something rotten going on here. Don't know what, but I intend to find out. Did you hear them talking?"

"Hear them?" replied Tom not understanding. "Of course not. But I heard that same chap you heard the other day—talking Dutch or something."

"That was them!" announced Rawlins decidedly. "Tom, they've got under-sea radio, too. It's those chaps we've been hearing, I'm beginning to get it. That word Oleander. That's a password—a countersign. Just as soon as they spoke it the door opened. There's some deep mystery here. What the deuce that torpedolike affair was I don't know. Perhaps they're trying to blow up some building. This sewer is under a busy part of the city. Hear those trucks and surface cars overhead?"

Absolutely dumbfounded, heedless of Frank's insistent but weak voice in his ears, striving to grasp all this astounding statement of Rawlins', Tom stood speechless for a moment. And then an idea flashed through his mind.

"Gosh!" he exclaimed. "Say, Mr. Rawlins, they'll find us. If they've got radio they can hear us too! Say, perhaps they're listening to us now. Come on, let's get out of here."

Rawlins' surprised whistle came shrilly to Tom's ears.

"You're right!" replied the diver. "We're in a dangerous place. Come on. Let me go first."

Crowding past Tom, Rawlins hurried as fast as the constantly deepening water and the darkness would permit and presently, though to Tom it seemed hours, a lighter space appeared ahead and a few moments later they once more were standing at the bottom of the river.

They had turned to retrace their steps towards their own dock and were following along the old wall when once more they were halted in their tracks. Again to their ears, borne to them by the radio waves, came the harsh foreign words.

So close did the words sound in their ears that instinctively, without stopping to think that the speakers might be hundreds of feet or even yards distant, the two crouched back in a recess of the masonry, flattening themselves against the slime-covered, weed-draped stones and gazing apprehensively towards the spot where the old sewer pierced the wall.

CHAPTER IX—THE BATTLE BENEATH THE RIVER

As they crouched there, Frank's voice was taking on a frightened tone and Tom could now hear it much more plainly. But Tom's mind was filled with the danger of being discovered and he scarcely dared reply, for somehow, although there was no foundation for his fears, he was filled with a terrible dread of these under-sea workers, these unknown mysterious divers who had lifted the ominous-looking metal cylinder through the trap-door in the disused sewer. That, even if they heard him and his friends, they could not trail them or locate them under water never occurred to him. In fact, he had quite forgotten that he and Rawlins were under water or were as invisible to others a few yards away as other objects were to them. He felt as though he could be as easily seen as if on land, and that, if he spoke, his words would at once betray his whereabouts. But he also realized that Frank's voice could be heard by others as well as by himself and so, steeling himself to the effort, he called back, "It's all right. Don't worry. Stop talking and listen."

Instantly, Frank's voice ceased and Tom drew a breath of relief and then he gulped and pressed close to Rawlins, for before him in the water, as if attracted by the sounds of his voice, the two dim forms of the strange divers once more appeared. For a space they remained motionless as though listening and perspiration broke out on Tom's forehead and chills ran up and down his spine as he heard distinctly the sounds of low-toned words in the same guttural tongue, and he was certain, positive, that his voice had been heard, that the others were striving to locate him, and that at any moment Frank or Henry might become curious or impatient and speak. In his terrified mind he could picture those big, sickly green, distorted beings creeping towards him, their wide-flung arms waving uncertainly like the tentacles of a huge octopus as they lurched forward; he could imagine the fixed, expressionless stare of those great goggle-eyed glasses in the squat neckless helmets and, as the current caused light and shadow to waver and change, the figures seemed actually moving towards his hiding place.

It was terrible; he no longer thought of them as fellow men, no longer looked upon them as human beings; his fears had transformed them to submarine monsters, weird, uncanny, intelligent but bloodthirsty creatures, and so great was the tension, so fearful the vision conjured up by his overwrought imagination that he would have screamed had his mouth not been parched and dry and incapable of uttering a sound. It was like a nightmare, a dream in which one is powerless to move or to cry out; where one cannot compel muscles or mind to function; where one feels that it cannot be real, cannot be possible and yet is filled with sweating, blood-curdling terror that it is. And then, after what seemed hours of torture, but was barely ten seconds from the time the men had emerged from the sewer, their voices ceased and to Tom's inexpressible relief they appeared to fade into the murky green water. They were moving away, soundlessly, mysteriously, without visible effort, and Tom noticed with his fright-filled eyes that above them was poised an indistinct, cigar-shaped object, the same torpedolike affair he had seen lifted from the sewer, and he realized that somehow, by some means, the men were dragging this along with them into the dim, green distance.

He was aroused by Rawlins' whisper and a touch on his arm.

"I'm going to follow," were the barely audible words. "No danger. Must see where they go. Come on."

Recovering from his fright, now that the divers were retreating, and rather reassured by the sound of his companion's voice and words Tom moved forward from the wall but still grasping Rawlins' hand.

They could not see the figures before them, for the muck stirred up by the others' passage concealed them as effectually as a smoke screen, but it also served to betray their whereabouts and to conceal Tom and Rawlins as well. For some distance— several hundred yards Tom thought—they moved along, following close to the wall that bounded the shore and ever with the slowly drifting column of muddy water to guide them.

Once or twice the murk seemed to drift away, and each time Rawlins instantly halted, waiting to see if those they were trailing had come to a stop, but each time the mud again rose before them and they resumed their way.

Tom had no idea of the distance or direction they had traveled. The effort he made to walk was his only guide and he knew that the same effort, the same number of steps on land, would have carried him a long way, but he also knew that under water his progress was snail-like, that a step might carry one a few inches or several feet or not at all, depending upon the current, and he wondered vaguely if Rawlins knew his way, if he could find his way back, or if he intended to bob to the surface to get his bearings when he finally decided to return to the dock. And Tom smiled to himself as he pictured the looks of surprise, the screams of fright which would greet their unexpected and sudden appearance if Rawlins did this and they should bob up beside some crowded recreation pier or ferry ship. But Rawlins had halted again.

Before them now the mud was thinning out, the water was being swept clear of silt and Rawlins drew Tom beside him behind a huge block of stone which had been dumped at the base of the wall. Slowly and gradually the water cleared. It was evident that those they were following were no longer stirring up the mud and so must have come to a stop and, as the sediment drifted off and the dim green light filtered through the water, Tom peered into the vast illimitable void. It was like looking through thick green glass or like glass made half-opaque by one's breath upon it and for a time Tom could see nothing. Then, as the water became still clearer, he saw the faint outlines of timbers and spiles and a dark object looming ominously, like a cloud, which he recognized as the bottom of some vessel. Against the lighter water over his head, a shadow passed and the greenness quivered and wavered and he knew a small boat was being rowed above them; but no sign could he see of those they had been following.

Then Tom noticed something else, something that rose above the dark bottom of the river as a darker mass, something that resembled a great bank of mud or a reef of rock. Irregular in outline, dark green as seen through the water, unlike anything he had ever seen, yet somehow it had a vaguely familiar look; it did not seem quite like mud or rock of any natural formation, but rather like some sort of boat. Yes, that was it—like the hull of a boat—it reminded him of a picture of a sunken wreck. Perhaps it was. Yes, now that the thought had entered his head, he could see that it was a wreck; he could make out the stump of a mast, the remains of deck houses, something like portions of rails. But what was it doing here? Why should a sunken hulk be lying in the East River? Of course it was out of the channel, it was lying partly beneath a dock or pier and Tom noticed that the spiles of the pier sagged and that several were broken off under water. Evidently the pier was an old one, perhaps disused, and maybe the old hulk had been sunk during some fire which had destroyed the pier at the same time.

All these thoughts flashed through Tom's mind as he peered into the dim greenness and then all were wiped from his brain as he caught a glimpse of the two divers moving from among the spiles. Tom was as much at sea as ever as to the distances under water. He could not tell whether the wreck was fifty or five hundred feet away. He was not at all sure that, if he reached out, he could not touch the old hulk or even the moving forms. The next moment the two had reached the side of the wreck and then, to Tom's amazement, they seemed to disappear within it, to step through the sides as though it were only a shadow in the water.

"Gosh," he ejaculated unconsciously, "they went into that wreck!"

"Wreck!" came Rawlins' whispered words. "Wreck! That's

no wreck. That's a submarine. That's their hangout!"

So absolutely thunderstruck was Tom at Rawlins' words that he could not even reply. But now he saw that what he had mistaken for a waterlogged sunken hulk was indeed an under-sea boat, a submarine and a big one. He had never seen a submarine except from above water before. He had no idea how such a craft would appear under water. He did not realize that the narrow deck almost awash, the tiny superstructure and conning tower which are all the landsman sees are but a very small portion of a submarine's whole; that out of sight, and never exposed above the surface of the sea, is a big boat-shaped hull with rudders and propellers; that the cigar-shaped Jules Verne type of submersible so familiar in fiction is not a thing of fact; and that the modern submarine if seen under water might easily be mistaken for an ordinary vessel's hull.

It was not at all surprising therefore that Tom had mistaken the submerged craft for the hulk of a steamer or ship, for submarines were the last thing in his mind and no one would have dreamed of seeing one here beneath the surface of the East River.

Now, however, Tom could see that what he had mistaken for the stump of a mast was the conning tower; what he had thought were shattered deck houses and rails were the superstructure; and he could now even make out the lateral horizontal rudders and the vertical rudder and screws.

But this made the mystery still greater. It was even more wonderful to find a submarine here than a sunken vessel. Of course, Tom knew there were plenty of the navy's submarines forever knocking about, and for an instant it occurred to him that it was one of these engaged in making some test and that the divers whom they had seen were members of the boat's crew.

Then instantly he remembered the men had spoken in a foreign tongue, that they had carried a mysterious object to the trapdoor in the sewer, and that they had taken the same or a duplicate object from the sewer.

It was all inexplicable, puzzling, unfathomable.

Rawlins' voice recalled him to the present.

"They've gone," said the diver. "I want to find out who and what she is. You stay here. I'll be away only a moment."

As he spoke, he released Tom's hand and with a final caution for the boy not to follow or move away, Rawlins floundered towards the submarine.

Interestedly Tom watched him. He noticed that Rawlins did not stir up the mud and then, for the first time, he discovered that the bottom was hard and sandy. Somehow all sense of fear and danger had left him. How foolish he had been, to be sure! No doubt, he thought to himself, it was the unexpected appearance of the men and their grotesque forms which had aroused his imagination. There was Rawlins, still moving away and looking as terrible and awesome as had the others—even more so, if anything, with his proboscis-like helmet topped by its grid and the container on his shoulders giving him the appearance of being humpbacked.

He wondered how far the submarine was from where he stood. Rawlins now seemed close to it and yet he could not possibly tell whether his friend was really near to the craft or not. It was all most interesting, most baffling and most unreal and dreamlike. He wondered what Frank and Henry would think of his long silence. He wondered if they could hear him or he could hear them. Surely there would be no danger in speaking now. Even if those in the submarine heard him they could not tell whether it was some one under or above the water who was speaking. Why hadn't he thought of that before? There never *had* been any danger. Of course, if these men had under-sea radio they must hear messages from those on land as well as the boys.

In that case they would never have had suspicions if they had overheard the boys' conversation. They would never dream that others possessed the apparatus and would have assumed that the speakers were on shore. There was no danger; he was sure of it, and he was about to call to Frank when his attention was arrested by Rawlins' actions.

Tom had been idly watching him and had seen him reach the submarine. He had seen Rawlins moving around the craft, evidently examining it, and he had lost sight of him as Rawlins had slipped around the blunt bow. But now Rawlins suddenly appeared, backing into view, waving his arms to maintain his balance and floundering. And he held something in one hand, something that he waved menacingly above his head, some object that glittered even in the dull, subdued, green light.

For the space of a second, Tom was puzzled and then he knew. It was Rawlins' hatchet! Something or some one was attacking him and scarcely had this knowledge flashed through Tom's mind when, from behind the submarine, the two figures appeared, clutching arms pawing at the water as if swimming, bodies bent far forward, their every attitude, every motion betokening speed, speaking of straining efforts to come within reach of Rawlins, despite his threatening, keen-edged hatchet.

Wildly excited, filled with deadly fear, terrorized at Rawlins' plight as was Tom, yet through his mind ran the thought, the subconscious feeling, that it was all unreal—a dream or a delusion. It was unspeakably and inexpressibly uncanny to see the three men evidently exerting every effort and yet moving so silently and slowly, seeming to float like weightless bodies in some semi-transparent, green medium. It reminded Tom of a slow motion picture—one of the films where a man or a horse, leaping a hurdle, appears to float lightly as a bit of thistledown through the air—and watching, the boy was fascinated. But only for the briefest moment.

Scarcely had the three come within Tom's view when Rawlins stumbled over an upjutting stub of spiling, the hatchet flew from his hand and before he could half rise the others were upon him.

At this, the spell was broken. Tom screamed aloud and the

next instant, like a voice from another sphere, he heard Frank speaking.

"What is the matter, Tom? What's wrong?" came in troubled, worried tones. "Why *did* you yell?"

Here then was help. They were still within reach of those ashore and in terse, excited, fear-wrung tones Tom answered.

"Help! Send for help!" he yelled, entirely forgetting that no one knew where he was or where to send help even if help could have reached them there under the river.

"It's awful!" he continued. "Two men—divers—from a submarine—fighting with Mr. Rawlins! They're attacking him—struggling with him! Get Dad, get the police!"

Then, faint and as from a vast distance, he heard Frank's voice calling excitedly for Mr. Pauling's telephone number. He knew his chum was summoning aid and he sat rigid, watching with staring eyes the struggle taking place beneath the river. Rawlins had arisen; by a tremendous effort he had flung aside one man, but the other was grappling with him, fighting desperately, and as Tom saw something flash in the water above the struggling men's heads he realized that the stranger held a knife.

Now they had drawn closer, they were some distance from the submarine and the very instant Tom noticed this a wild cry of alarm rang in his ears.

At the sound, Tom saw one man start to plunge towards the under-sea boat, and to the boy's astonishment he saw that the craft was moving and was slipping rapidly from its resting place. Although the man struggled desperately to reach it he might as well have stood still, for scarcely did Tom realize that the submarine was under way ere it was a mere shadow and a second later had faded into the murky green.

And now Tom saw that Rawlins was the aggressor, the man who had been chasing the submarine was swaying drunkenly, whirling in a half-circle, his arms waving helplessly, while his companion had broken away from Rawlins and was standing, with hands upraised, and backing slowly away from the latter who leaned towards him with the other's knife in his hand.

"Kamarad!" Tom heard in thick tones. "Kamarad!" and the boy's heart jumped as he heard the words of surrender, the words which had become so familiar to thousands of men in the trenches, and Tom, with a shock of surprise, realized that the divers were Germans.

Now he could hear Rawlins' words, spoken as if to himself or as if he thought the others could hear.

"Yes, you dirty skunk!" Tom caught. "I'll tell the world you'll surrender. All right, right about face and forward march and no nonsense or I'll puncture that suit and your hide under it."

And then Tom's brain had another sudden jolt. Of course the German could hear. Of course Rawlins had heard his cry of surrender. What a dolt he had been! They had radio sets, they could hear everything that was said as readily as he could. That was why they had given up the fight, yes that was it, that was why the submarine had cleared out. They had heard his cry for help, had heard him tell Frank to summon police. How could they know that their whereabouts was not known, that it was mere chance that he and Rawlins had stumbled upon them? No doubt they imagined they had been watched, trailed and surrounded and the submarine, rather than run the risk of being captured, had deserted the two men at the first sound of alarm being given. It was all clear to Tom now. The battle was over. Rawlins was victorious, the men were his prisoners. Now Rawlins was speaking again and Tom saw that the second man was being half-dragged along by his fellow. But Rawlins' words aroused Tom to instant activity.

"Are you all right, Tom?" asked Rawlins. "Come over here. We need a hand. This chap's hurt somehow. Can't get an answer out of him. Short circuited or something. We've got to get him out somehow."

Lunging forward, Tom bumped into Rawlins before he had

taken six steps and gave a startled exclamation. Was it possible the fight had taken place so close? But he had no time to think on this matter. The second man was helpless, dead, as far as appearances went, and Rawlins, stooping quickly, cut the lead-soled boots from his feet.

Thus relieved of the weights, the body partly floated and with Tom holding to one arm and the captured man grasping the other, while Rawlins kept a hand on Tom and directed the way, the strange under-sea procession floundered through the water, along the wall, past the black sewer mouth and towards Rawlins' dock.

And now Tom again heard Frank's voice.

"Where are you?" it asked. "Your father's coming. How can they find you? Are you all right?"

"Everything's all right," answered Tom. "We're coming back. Be there soon!"

Hardly a minute later, Tom saw the familiar piers near their own dock. He had thought they had wandered far, but they had not been two hundred yards distant at any time. A moment later, they reached the foot of the ladder.

Telling Tom to go up, Rawlins half lifted the unconscious man and with a gruff warning to his fellow started to mount the rungs. Evidently the words were heard by the anxious, waiting boys above, for Tom heard Frank's shout of joy and he called back as he drew himself towards the open trap.

But before his head emerged from the water, a crash like thunder sounded in his ears, there was a sound of tramping, hurrying footsteps, shouts and cries and Tom's brain reeled. What was happening? Had the men's confederates learned of their capture? Were their fellows breaking into the laboratory to rescue them? Were the ruffians wreaking vengeance on Frank and Henry?

CHAPTER X—RADIO WINS

As the confused sounds, the crash, the tramp of rushing feet, the excited men's voices and Frank's high-pitched tones came dimly to Tom's ears, a deadly sickening fear swept over him. Had they escaped the men from the submarine only to fall into the clutches of their confederates?

He had been under a tremendous strain, he had been terribly frightened, his heart had been almost bursting with excitement and he had been under water for much longer than ever before. The combination was too much for him. His head swam, he reeled, swayed; fiery sparks and flashes seemed to dance before his eyes; he felt a numbness stealing over him. Wildly he clutched at the ladder in a last despairing effort and seemed sinking, slowly, softly into a vast billowy void.

He opened his eyes and uttered a surprised cry. He was lying on the floor of the laboratory and his father, anxious-eyed, was bending over him while close at hand were Frank, Henry and Rawlins. Beyond and as a confused mass Tom's eyes saw blue-clad figures and with a start he rose to a sitting posture.

"Gosh!" he exclaimed, staring about and for the moment not comprehending. "What's the matter, Dad? What's happened?"

"Are you all right, Tom?" asked Mr. Pauling. "We got you just in time. You fainted just as you reached the ladder top. Don't you remember?"

Tom's senses had now fully returned.

"Yes, Dad," he replied. "I do now. Did Mr. Rawlins tell you about it? Gee! We *did* have a time! Are those men here?"

"Safe and sound, Tom!" Mr. Henderson's voice assured him. "That is, one of 'em is. The other's in bad shape."

"Yes, Rawlins told us something of what happened," put in his father as Tom rose unsteadily to his feet. "Look out, Son! You're weak yet. Sit down or you'll go off again."

Leaning on his father's arm, Tom staggered to the proffered chair and dropped weakly into it. Then he gazed about the room and at the crowd of men within it.

His father and Mr. Henderson, Rawlins, Frank and Henry

were there. Near-by, was a strange, heavy-jawed man and beyond, near the door, were half a dozen policemen. But where were the two divers they had captured under the river? Then Tom saw that a heavily built, tow-headed man stood between two of the blue coats, his hands manacled and a sullen glare in his piglike eyes while, half hidden beyond two stooping men, was a form stretched upon the floor. But before he could form a question his father was giving quick sharp orders to the men.

"Get the Navy Yard!" he commanded, and as the heavy-jawed man jumped to the telephone, he snapped out: "Tell the commandant that Pauling's speaking." Then, before the operator had even asked the number, Mr. Pauling was uttering commands to the police. "Leave a couple of men here to guard the prisoners and get over to that block quick as you can. Get all available men you can pick up. Draw a cordon around it and don't let any one in or out. Take my car! It's up to you fellows to nab this bunch—if they haven't got wise. On the jump now, Reilly! Take every one and everything that seems suspicious! Get me?"

Even before his last word rang out the policemen were hurrying towards the street, and an instant later, Tom heard the roar of their motor and the clang of their bell as the patrol dashed off.

"Navy Yard on the wire!" announced the man at the phone and Mr. Pauling grabbed the receiver.

"This is Pauling!" he announced shortly. "That you, Admiral? All right! Got important matter."

Then, to Tom's amazement, his father broke into the most utter gibberish, calling out a confused but rapid list of figures and words.

"That's done!" he exclaimed, as he slammed back the receiver and turned towards Tom. "There'll be a dozen destroyers and chasers combing the sea for that sub within fifteen minutes." Then, with a different note in his voice, he asked, "Do you feel all right, Son?"

As Tom answered, his father turned towards the men bending above the figure on the floor. "Come here when you have a chance, Doctor," he called. "Want you to have a look at my boy."

At his words, one of the men rose and hurried to Tom's side.

"Had a close call, my boy!" he exclaimed, as he took Tom's wrist and drew out his watch. "Good thing Rawlins fixed up these suits so you couldn't inhale flames. Different case with that chap yonder. He's in bad shape. Trying to fix him up to get him to hospital. Afraid there's no hope for him though! Oh, you're O. K. Fit as a fiddle! Pulse fine! Nothing wrong with him, Pauling. Just a bit of nerves, I expect, and strain of being down too long."

Hurrying from Tom's side he again devoted himself to the injured man.

Things were moving so rapidly that Tom was dazed and was striving his best to gather his wits together and to understand all that was taking place. Mr. Henderson and Rawlins were talking earnestly in low tones, but Tom could not hear a word they said and was busy replying to his father's, Henry's and Frank's questions and plying them with queries in turn.

Presently Rawlins and Mr. Henderson rose and as the former came to Tom's side the other strode across the room and, facing the prisoner, stared fixedly into his face.

"I guess you're all right, Tom," said Rawlins, the tone of his voice betraying far more solicitude than was conveyed by his words. "You're some kid, I'll tell the world! You'll be famous if you don't watch out. Say, old man, I'm mighty sorry I kept you down so long. Never thought about you not being accustomed to it. I was so darned interested in that sub and those men I forgot about the danger to you, Tom. And say, Mr. Henderson thinks we've made some haul! I've been telling him the whole yarn— the Dutch talk and all the rest. Henderson thinks he recognizes that Hun we brought up and sees a big plot behind all this. Too bad the other fellow got flames and can't talk. Your radio's all to the mustard, I'll say!"

At this moment Mr. Henderson's voice interrupted them. As he had stared searchingly but silently at the prisoner the latter's shifty eyes had fallen and he shuffled his feet uneasily. Then, without warning and so suddenly Tom and the others jumped, Henderson snapped out:

"Open your mouth!"

So unexpected was the command that the prisoner, long trained to instant and implicit obedience to orders, involuntarily threw back his head opened his enormous mouth.

"Thought so!" ejaculated Mr. Henderson and then, even before the surprised man's jaws closed, he yanked aside the fellow's denim shirt exposing the hairy freckled chest with a livid white scar diagonally across it.

"That's enough!" snapped out Mr. Henderson. Then, addressing Tom's father he remarked, "It's he, Pauling. No question of it. Good day's work this—thanks to Rawlins' suits and Tom's under-sea radio."

"Wha-what's it all about?" demanded Tom, absolutely at a loss to grasp the meaning of all the orders, the strange telephone message and Mr. Henderson's statements. "Who *are* the men and *what* were they doing?"

"Never mind now," replied his father. "We'll get home first. Feel ready to go?"

"Oh, I'm all right now," declared Tom. "Only a bit tired out."

"Call for a couple of plain-clothes men to stay here," Mr. Pauling ordered, turning towards the heavy-jawed man. "Don't want any one meddling with the instruments. Keep that trap shut and bolted and don't sleep on the job."

Then, to the surgeons, "Soon as he comes to and can talk, call me up. If he says anything, write it down. Don't let any one—any one, mind you—speak with him."

The surgeon nodded in assent and as the other man again

went to the telephone Mr. Pauling and Rawlins half lifted Tom, and, accompanied by Frank, Henry and Mr. Henderson, the party left the workshop. Already the two policemen had left with their prisoner and were pressing through a curious crowd which had gathered outside and which was held in check by more stalwart, blue-coated men.

"Gosh! you've got the whole of the New York police here!" exclaimed Tom.

"Not quite that," laughed his father, "but Henderson surely did call enough of them. Guess they thought we were going to raid a liner."

"Well, you didn't name any limit," replied Mr. Henderson chuckling. "You said 'call the police' and I called 'em. Might as well be on the safe side, you know."

As Mr. Pauling helped Tom into Mr. Henderson's car he saw the man whom Rawlins had captured in his spectacular battle under the river being shoved into a patrol wagon.

"Do tell me who he is," begged Tom. "Is he a German spy?"

His father laughed. "You've forgotten the war's over and done with and there are no spies," he replied. "No, my boy, he's not even a German. But you'll have to wait a bit before I can tell you anything more."

"Well, where did you send those policemen, then?" asked Tom. "You can tell me that."

Mr. Pauling's eyes twinkled. "They've gone to get your phantom radio man," he replied. "Henderson's men couldn't find him before, but I'll wager we located him this time. You see, Reilly happened to know about that old sewer and he says it runs under the block where you located the sender of those odd messages. Henderson thinks if he finds one he'll find the other. We'll run around past there and see if anything is happening."

As Frank and Henry crowded into the little car, the boys saw a stretcher bearing a shrouded form being carried from their workshop to an ambulance, and the next moment they were moving slowly through the crowd which reluctantly made way before the insistent screams of the horn.

Close behind them came another car with Mr. Henderson and Rawlins and a moment later they were through the crowd and speeding towards the block to which Mr. Pauling had dispatched the police.

As they swung around a corner they saw a surging, densely packed throng blocking the street, while from beyond came the sounds of shouts and cries. Above the heads of the people the boys could see the glaring brass and shining paint of two patrol cars and, moving here and there, rising and falling as if tossed about upon a troubled sea, the low-visored, flat-topped caps of policemen.

"Can't get through there!" declared Mr. Pauling, as his horn screeched and fell on unheeding ears. "Looks like a riot!"

Mr. Henderson had leaped from his car and was beside them. "Guess the men found something," he remarked. "I'll push through and see what's up."

With Rawlins by his side, he wedged his way into the crowd and the two were instantly swallowed up. But a moment later they reappeared, hats and collars awry, coats torn open, and panting.

"Whew!" exclaimed Mr. Henderson. "Might as well try to get through a solid wall. Hello! There's another wagon!"

As he spoke, a bell clanged harshly and above the heads of the mob a car crowded with police could be seen forcing its way towards the center of the disturbance which appeared to be a large garage.

At this moment a huge, lumbering motor truck crept slowly from the garage door and an angry bellow rose from the crowd. But even an East Side mob must give way before a five-ton truck and the crowd, surging back to make way for the truck, swept around the boys and the two cars and engulfed them like a sea of rough clothes and angry, grimy faces.

"How the dickens can we get clear now!" exclaimed Mr. Henderson, as to save themselves from being knocked down and trampled underfoot he and Rawlins leaped upon the running boards and flattened themselves against the body of the car.

"Expect we'll have to stick here until the crowd leaves," replied Mr. Pauling, and added, "Unless they pick us up car and all and carry us out."

Now the crowd was surging still farther back as though pressed by an irresistible force and above the bellowing, moving, multicolored wave of human heads and shoulders appeared a half-dozen mounted police, their well-trained horses forcing back the human wall which, despite jeers, taunts, threats and imprecations, gave way steadily before them.

As the police drew near and the crowd thinned out, one of the officers caught sight of the two cars and their occupants.

"Here you!" he shouted, urging his horse towards the car. "Get them flivvers out o' here! Right about now and move lively!"

Mr. Pauling chuckled and Mr. Henderson grinned. "Show us how!" cried back Mr. Pauling.

"No sassing back there!" stormed the policeman now riding close. "Get a move on or I'll pinch the bunch of ye for interferin' with the police, resistin' an officer and blockadin' traffic. I'll get enough charges against ye to send youse to the island for a year."

Mr. Henderson and Tom's father were shaking with laughter. "Don't be foolish, officer. Don't you see we can't move?" Mr. Henderson asked.

The policeman's face grew purple with anger and he pushed his mount close beside the car, calling to a fellow officer to help him.

Exasperated by the crowd, naturally quick-tempered and in a frenzy of rage at these "swells," as he mentally dubbed them, defying his orders, he drew his club and raised it threateningly.

Mr. Henderson leaped from the running board to the policeman's side and in tones which even the angry blue coat recognized as authoritative exclaimed,

"Here, that's enough from you! You'll find yourself broke if you don't look out. Your job's to protect citizens—not to abuse them!"

A look of mingled amazement and anger swept over the officer's face.

"An' who may youse be?" he began, hunching himself forward and shooting forth his pugnacious jaw.

Mr. Henderson stepped a bit closer and turned back the lapel of his vest.

The sudden change in the man's attitude and expression caused the boys to burst out laughing. Surprise, incredulity, fear, and regret all spread over his big Hibernian features in turn. His half-raised arm dropped to his side, he seemed to shrivel and shrink in size, his pale blue eyes seemed about to pop from between his red-lashed lids.

Then Irish humor came to his rescue. Drawing himself stiffly up he saluted and with a twinkle in his eyes blurted out,

"B'gorra, Sir, 'tis sorry I am. But how was I to know, Sir? What with your kelly dinted in and your tie adrift and all. Sure I'll see ye through here in a jiffy."

The crowd had now been driven far back, and, escorted by the mounted men, the two cars proceeded slowly up the street until opposite the garage. A few idlers were still hovering about and were being chased away by blue coats, but inside the garage the boys could see a closely packed mass of men with policemen's caps much in evidence, while the broad doorway was blocked by officers with drawn clubs.

As Mr. Pauling brought his car to a stop, a plain-clothes man pressed through the line of police and hurried to the car.

"What's up?" demanded Mr. Pauling as the man came close. "Find anything?"

"Find anything!" repeated the other, his gimlet eyes fairly glistening with satisfaction. "You bet your—beg your pardon—I'll say we did. Got the whole bunch—men, cars, booze an' all. Want the story now?"

"No, don't stop now, Murphy," replied Mr. Pauling, "After everything's cleaned up come around to the house and we'll hear the whole yarn, the boys are entitled to know it. I'm expecting a call to the hospital at any time and must be on hand. Glad you got them."

"I guess I'll stay and see the fun," said Rawlins, "that is, if I may."

"Let Mr. Rawlins in, Murphy," commanded Mr. Pauling. "He's one of our crowd and all right. Wouldn't have got this job over without his help. See you later."

As the car drove off, the boys saw Rawlins pushing through the cordon of police by Murphy's side and all three breathed a sigh of regret that they, too, could not remain to see what exciting and interesting things were taking place within the garage.

But they realized that it was no place for boys and, to tell the truth, all three were quite ready and willing to go home and have a chance to calm down and rest. Tom, of course, had been through a racking experience and was utterly exhausted nervously and physically, and Frank, who was younger and of a far more nervous temperament, had been so worried and frightened over Tom's plight and the uncertainty of what was occurring under the water that he had become almost hysterical when it was all over. Even Henry had experienced enough excitement to last him for some time and boylike was crazy to rush home and tell his parents all about the remarkable adventures of the afternoon.

Leaving Henry at Gramercy Square, Mr. Pauling drove the car home while Mr. Henderson went to his office and Tom and Frank, who was staying at the Pauling home while his parents were in Europe, breathed a sigh of satisfaction when they found themselves once more in the cool, quiet interior of the house on Madison Avenue.

CHAPTER XI—HENDERSON HAS AN INTERVIEW

When, after parting with Mr. Pauling and the boys, Mr. Henderson drove towards his office, he was in high good humor. The afternoon, thanks to the boys' radio and Rawlins' diving suits, had been a most eventful and highly satisfactory one. Not only had the discoveries resulted in the raid on the garage, the seizure of a vast amount of contraband and probably the breaking up of the gang of rum-runners which for so long had baffled his men and himself, but it had brought in two prisoners, one of whom at least he had recognized and was mighty glad to see.

But despite all this he was sorely puzzled and cudgeled his brain to find a reasonable explanation for many things which seemed inexplicable. If, as it seemed, the garage had been a hiding place for smuggled liquor, what connection did it have with the submarine and the divers Rawlins had captured? Had the contraband been brought there in the under-seas boat, and if so how? He knew, as Rawlins had already pointed out, that a submarine could not go in and out of any port—in the West Indies or elsewhere—without attracting immediate attention, for there were not many of the craft knocking about and even if the natives of the islands had kept the secret some of the government's agents who were scattered through the West Indies would either have seen or heard of the craft. Mr. Pauling, for example, had personally been to Cuba and Nassau and while he had seen schooners leave with cargoes only to return empty without being reported from any American port, still he had found or heard nothing which would indicate a submarine unless, yes, that might be possible—the schooners might have transferred their cargoes to the under-sea boat in mid-ocean or at some uninhabited island.

But even in that case, the native sailors, the mulattoes and negroes, surely would have talked about it. To them, a submarine would have been far too remarkable and interesting a thing not to have told their wondering cronies and families about it. And where, assuming this was so, had the bootleggers secured the vessel?

Rawlins had assured him the submarine was a German U-boat of a recent type, such as had been off the United States coast during the latter days of the war, but she could not be one of these, for the Navy, he knew, had accounted for them all. Had the Germans taken to rum-running? Had they secretly retained one or more submarines, and, knowing the enormous profits to be made, put them to use carrying cargoes of liquor from the West Indies to the United States? Of course this was possible, but somehow Mr. Henderson, who was famed in the Service for his "hunches," which nine-tenths of the time proved right, had a feeling that there was something deeper, some mystery behind it, and he had high hopes of fathoming this or at least of throwing some light upon it by an interview with the unharmed prisoner.

That he would obtain a confession or even much information from the fellow, he very much doubted, for he knew the man of old—knew him for a sullen, arrogant and thoroughly desperate man and one who could and did keep his mouth shut under the most severe grilling. Mr. Henderson deeply regretted that the other prisoner had been injured by inhaling the flames in his helmet, for with two men, each thinking the other had betrayed him, there would be a good chance of getting at the bottom of things, but it was almost hopeless now. The surgeons had stated that the man was doomed, that he could not possibly survive his terrible burns and that it was doubtful if he ever regained consciousness. Mr. Pauling was to be summoned when the wounded man came to his senses, if he ever did, and in the meantime the other prisoner was to be brought before Mr.

Henderson by two of his own men whom he had despatched for the purpose, for, while he and Mr. Pauling coöperated with the police in many ways, they had no desire to let the police learn of many matters that were taking place or hear statements or confessions which they might repeat.

As soon as Mr. Henderson reached his office, where the erstwhile janitor was on guard, he hurried the latter off and then, taking some documents from a safe and lighting his pipe, he proceeded to study the papers with minute attention. He was interrupted in this by the return of the messenger who was accompanied by a small, wiry, dark-haired man whom Mr. Henderson addressed as "Ivan" and who seated himself in a proffered chair and proceeded to make himself quite at home with an immense black cigar.

"It's Smernoff!" announced Mr. Henderson presently. "Got him to-day under very remarkable circumstances—no matter what. Recognized him at once although he's shaved off his beard. Examined his mouth and chest to make sure. I expect him here in a few moments. Do you happen to know if he ever served in the German army?"

"Sure, yes, I know," replied the Russian. "Not in the army, no, but the navy."

"What was his job?" demanded Mr. Henderson.

"That I do not know," replied the other with a shrug of his shoulders.

"H-m-m," muttered Mr. Henderson. "Well, I want you to be here to interpret. He doesn't speak much English or won't. I guess they're coming now."

A moment later, there was a rap on the door and the janitor—once more in jumper and overalls—left by another entrance and armed with dustpan and broom proceeded to busy himself in the hallway exactly as if he had not been interrupted several hours previously by Frank's excited summons to Mr. Pauling.

At Mr. Henderson's "Come in!" two heavily built men in

civilian clothes entered, crowding closely one on either side of the sullen man who had been captured by Rawlins.

Not until they had seated themselves at Mr. Henderson's orders would any one have suspected that the pig-eyed man was a prisoner or was handcuffed. For a space, Mr. Henderson gazed steadily and silently at the prisoner who returned his stare, hate and venom in his eyes, and then, turning to Ivan, Mr. Henderson ordered him to ask the fellow certain questions.

It is not necessary to repeat the conversation, or rather the queries and replies, and for some time no satisfactory information was brought out, the captive absolutely refusing to admit anything or to say a word which might incriminate himself or his fellows. But when, after a deal of questioning, Mr. Henderson had Ivan hint that the men captured in the raid on the garage had betrayed the Russian and his fellow diver, the man's face took on a demoniacal expression, his eyes blazed and a torrent of curses and foul oaths burst from his lips.

A moment later, he checked his furious outburst and replied quickly to many of the interrogations put to him through the interpreter.

It was soon evident, however, that he was either extremely ignorant of many matters or else was an accomplished liar, and, while the information he gave cleared up many matters which had puzzled Mr. Henderson previously, still the most important and mysterious features of the whole case remained as much a mystery as ever.

"I guess that's all we can find out, or all he'll tell," declared Mr. Henderson at last. "Take him away and be mighty careful to have him well guarded. He's a slippery rascal and we don't want him getting away this time."

As the men with their prisoner left the room, Ivan rose as if to go.

"Sit down!" Mr. Henderson ordered him. "I may need you again at any minute. We've got another man to question yet."

Ivan's eyebrows rose in surprise, but he had long been employed as an interpreter in Mr. Pauling's service and had learned not to ask questions or make comments, no matter how amazing or perplexing a matter might appear. So, again seating himself comfortably, he lit another of his huge cigars and waited patiently and silently for further orders.

Meanwhile Mr. Henderson was going over his hastily written statements of the prisoner and with his knowledge of the man's past and his "hunch" was striving to dovetail the information with surmises and records so as to form a complete whole.

It was interesting and fascinating work—this building up a case from fragments and conjectures—a sort of jig-saw puzzle with many of the parts missing, and Mr. Henderson was an adept at it. Indeed, he often spent hours, when he had time to spare, playing the game with imaginary or hypothetical cases exactly as a person will play a game of solitaire. It was this ability to piece together stray bits of evidence, and his almost uncanny intuition, that had secured the high position he held and had won the envy and admiration of all in the Service who knew him, although his friends good-naturedly chaffed him about his "imagination," as they called it.

But on more than one occasion his imagination, or intuition or sixth sense or whatever it might be, had brought most astonishing results; as, for example, the capture of a band of plotters; to which he had referred when discussing the flood of Bolshevist literature and the wave of crime with his coworkers.

Now, as he studied his notes of Smernoff's statements and at times half closed his eyes as if concentrating on some far-off matter, a smile spread across his features and from time to time he nodded approvingly.

"I'd wager it is," he commented to himself. "Everything points that way. The submarine, Smernoff—a fanatical socialist—those remarkable deep-sea suits—the under-sea radio, the mystery about it all and yes—the time hitches perfectly. Bloody sort of brute he is—wish I could get him for that—sorry it's out of our hands. Jove! I hope that mate of his lives long enough to give us what we want. Smernoff admits *he* knows. By Jove, it would be a coup! Wonder if those boys even dream what their experimenting has led up to!"

He was still deeply engrossed in his occupation when the phone bell rang and Mr. Pauling's voice came to him. "He's conscious," said the latter, "Come to the hospital as quickly as possible. Yes, I'm going this instant. Of course. Bring Ivan."

"Come along, Ivan!" exclaimed Mr. Henderson, as he hung up the receiver, and grasping his hat he hurried from the room into which the janitor instantly popped like some sort of automaton.

As soon as the ambulance bearing the injured prisoner had reached the hospital, the man had been taken to a private room and the doctors had devoted every attention, every latest appliance, every resource known to modern medicine and surgery to patching the horribly burned and disfigured fellow up in order to prolong his life until he could regain consciousness. In the hospital a more thorough examination had revealed the fact that the interior of his mouth was not so seriously burned as had been thought when first aid was being administered at the dock. Evidently he had had presence of mind enough to snap off the valve and to shut his lips at the first burst of flames from the chemicals when, startled by the submarine deserting them, he had instinctively cried out a warning to his mate and had allowed water to enter the tube.

"There's about one chance in ten thousand that he may live," announced the gray-haired surgeon to his assistant. "He has not inhaled flames and it all depends upon his constitution. The shock was enough to kill an ordinary man outright, but it will be no kindness to have him survive. If it were not for Mr. Pauling's orders I'd take the responsibility of letting him go, I believe. Gad! Can you imagine any one living with a face like that or caring enough to live to undergo the agony that he'll suffer if he becomes conscious?"

"Not me!" replied the younger man. "I'd think it a Christian act to let cases of this sort find relief in death, but I suppose every man has a right to his life if he wants it. Have any idea why Mr. Pauling's so keen on having him come to and talk?"

The elder man gazed at his assistant in a peculiar manner.

"No!" he snapped out at last. "And I'm not fool enough to ask or wonder. It's none of our business and I intend to follow orders to the letter. But you can bet it's something important. Just peep outside the door."

With a puzzled expression, the young doctor opened the door cautiously and looked to left and right. On either hand, standing silently, but with watchful eyes, were two heavily built men, dressed in civilian clothes, with soft, dark felt hats on their heads and, even to the intern's unpracticed eyes, detectives.

"Guess there *is* something doing," he remarked as he closed the door, "couple of Bulls out there. What do they think—that he's going to jump up and run with that face and with both eyes burned out?"

The other glanced up from where he was bending close above the cot and raised a finger for silence. Then, an instant later, he straightened up.

"Get Mr. Pauling at once!" he commanded. "Tell him the man is liable to become conscious at any instant—that he may live, but if he wants to be sure he had better come immediately."

In the mean time, at the Pauling home, Tom had been relating his story of the strange and exciting events which had taken place under the river.

"Now, Son," said Mr. Pauling, as Tom had thrown himself upon the lounge in the library while his mother hovered anxiously over him, "if you feel able, tell us all about it. Rawlins told us the main facts while you were getting over your fainting spell, but, as many important matters and far-reaching consequences may result from your discoveries and captures, I would like to know all the details. Just as soon as you feel tired, stop. Your health and welfare are the most important things—everything else can wait if necessary. I would not ask you now, only I know your mother is anxious to hear the story and, moreover, if I am called to the hospital, I would like to have as much information as possible. A lot may hinge on that."

"Oh, I'm quite all right, Dad," Tom assured his father. "Of course I'm tired, but I don't mind talking. In fact I'd like to."

So, for some time, Tom narrated his adventures, beginning with the descent to test the set at a distance and ending with the crash that sounded in his ears as he was about to emerge from the water and leaving out no detail of his sensations, thoughts or fears.

"I think it's all quite clear," declared Mr. Pauling when he had finished. "I'm sorry I cannot divulge everything to you now or explain all the mysteries which surround the astounding discovery that you boys and Mr. Rawlins have made. But later I can and will, as I know you must be dying of curiosity. And I can assure you of one thing: Uncle Sam will be under a great obligation to you and your radio."

"But you said you'd tell us who the man was whom we captured and what they were doing in the garage," Tom reminded him.

"Yes, I can do that," replied his father, "but you two boys must learn to keep secrets and not repeat anything I tell you. The man you and Rawlins brought in—the one who was not hurt I mean—is a Russian, a rabid 'red,' and Henderson recognized him and later identified him beyond question by a peculiar tooth and the scar on his chest. At one time he was convicted of a serious crime against our government, but escaped mysteriously from prison. I doubt very much if we get much information from him, as he knows he must serve out his term—with a bit added to it—and he is a close-mouthed rascal. We hope more from his companion, if he recovers consciousness and can talk.

If he knows he is dying he may confess at the last minute. As far as the garage is concerned, as you know, we put two and two together and decided the blind sewer had some secret opening in the block where you boys located the mysterious sending set. The fact that both those messages and the conversations you heard under water included the names of flowers convinced us that they emanated from the same source and as Rawlins assured us the conversation in what he called Dutch, but which was probably Russian, came from the men under water, it confirmed our suspicions that the man you boys located was talking to men under water or on the submarine and that somewhere in the block we would find the key to the mystery and more. From what Murphy says, and the appearance of things, we succeeded beyond our expectations. I was afraid that the rascals might have overheard you and Rawlins or that the submarine, which evidently knew that they were discovered, might have warned them. If so, we moved too quickly for them."

"But *are* they bootleggers?" asked Frank.

"No doubt," replied Mr. Pauling, "and many other worse things. When Murphy and Rawlins arrive we'll probably know more and if the wounded man confesses we'll solve many mysteries which remain to be unraveled."

"Well, I'm mighty glad the old under-sea radio worked," declared Tom, "but I wouldn't go through that experience again, not for—no, not for Uncle Sam himself."

At this moment the doorbell rang and a moment later Rawlins dashed into the room, his eyes bright and a happy grin on his boyish face.

"I'll tell the world it's great!" he exclaimed, "They got pretty near everything—booze, trucks, men, and that mysterious radio. And a truckload of books and papers—cleaned out a regular nest. That man Murphy is a corker, Mr. Pauling. He said to tell you he'll be over in a little while. They were just cleaning up when I left."

Tom jumped up. "Hurrah!" he cried. "Then we were right all along! We always said that fellow was one of a bootlegger gang. Gee, Frank! They can't laugh at radio or radio detectives now. It wins!"

"I'll say radio wins!" cried Rawlins.

CHAPTER XII—THE CONFESSION

Before the conversation could be continued, the desk telephone rang and Mr. Pauling instantly answered.

"Hello!" the boys heard him say. "Hello! Good! Right away. Call Henderson. Yes, have everything ready. He'll live perhaps? Yes, Henderson will bring Ivan. Keep a record of everything. Good-by!"

As he ceased speaking, Mr. Pauling sprang up. "It's Doctor Hewlett," he announced as he started for the door, "The man's regaining consciousness. He may talk at any moment and I must rush there. If Murphy calls, send him over."

An instant later, Mr. Pauling was hurrying to his car and the boys, Mrs. Pauling and Rawlins commenced discussing the events which had followed one another so rapidly during the past few hours.

Rawlins had to tell the story all over again to Tom's mother and Frank gave his version. Then all speculated on what the mystery surrounding the submarine and the raid on the garage might be.

"It's rather too bad that Fred can't tell us anything yet," said Mrs. Pauling, "but I realize, in his position, secrecy must be maintained. However, after it's all over I suppose we shall know—that is, if the newspapers don't tell us first. They usually manage to find out such secrets somehow."

"Well, I admit I can't see head nor tail to it," declared Rawlins. "Of course, as long as Mr. Pauling says those chaps are Russians and were talking Bolshevik I suppose they are and were; but I *know* that sub was a Hun boat—not one of the big, latest U-boats, but the kind that was over on our coast here once or twice. I've done a lot of work studying submarines and they can't fool me. Now, of course there's no reason why a Russian should not use a German sub if he could get hold of it, but what were they doing over here in the East River is what gets me. I don't believe they were just rum-runners, even if Murphy and his crowd did find a lot of booze over there, and what was that cigar-shaped sub-sea gadget they were pulling along with 'em?"

"Why, I think that's all simple," declared Tom. "They probably brought liquor in here with the submarine and carried it to the garage in that torpedolike thing."

Rawlins shook his head. "No, old man," he replied. "A sub would never do for a rum-runner. Why, every port in the West Indies is watched and the whole world would hear if a sub poked her nose into a harbor and tied up to a dock to load rum. It's too bad we didn't tackle those chaps out there before they got to the sub. We might have brought in that torpedo arrangement, too."

"Gee, I'd forgotten all about that!" exclaimed Tom. "What became of it?"

"Why, didn't I tell you?" replied Rawlins. "They shoved it into the submarine. I was watching 'em do that when they spotted me. If they'd had sense they'd have gone in after it and cleared out, but instead, they had to try rough-house stuff and got left. I expect they thought we'd seen too much and didn't know I was armed. Then, when their mates in the sub heard you yelling for help and heard Frank's replies, they thought the game was up and pulled stakes without stopping for the two chaps below."

"I wonder if they'll get her—the destroyers, I mean," said Frank.

"I doubt it," replied Rawlins. "The sea's a mighty big place and the Lord knows where she'll emerge. No knowing which way she headed either. For all any one knows she may have scooted over to some hangout on Long Island or swung around up the Hudson or slipped into the sound or stood out to sea. But I doubt if she'll try getting out of the harbor submerged. Too risky. She might bump into a liner or a ship any minute and she'd have to go blind—no periscope out, you see, because she'll know we'd have chasers, looking for her. No, I expect they'll submerge, rest on the bottom in shallow water somewhere and wait until night. Then she could sneak out to sea with just her conning tower out. There's about one chance in a million of finding her and that's the only way we slipped up. Just as soon as I saw her I knew something crooked was going on—knew it soon as ever I put eyes on those fellows in self-contained suits—infringing my patents, darn 'em—and I planned to get back and notify the authorities. Then we could have nabbed her and her whole crew. Slipped up by letting those Bolshevik birds spot me. And Tom—did you notice those fellows didn't have those gadgets on their helmets? How do you suppose they worked their radio without 'em?"

"Gosh!" exclaimed Tom. "I didn't think of it at the time, but it's so. Say, what became of their suits? We can examine their outfits and find out all about it."

"Suits are safe enough down at the dock," Rawlins assured him. "You'll have some fun examining them, I'll say."

"Why didn't you ask Mr. Murphy all about what it meant?" inquired Frank, who had been pondering on the mystery.

Rawlins gave a hearty laugh. "You don't know friend Murphy," he answered. "I'll say I asked him, but you might as well ask a lamp-post. I know why they call potatoes Murphys now—all eyes and no mouth. That's him, too. Nice and pleasant and everything, but not a mite of information. When I asked him first time he just looked me all over as if I was some kind of a rare specimen. 'Mr. Pauling says youse is on the level,' he said, 'and I'll take his word if he says the devil himself has turned saint. But my orders is to say nothing to nobody till I reports to Mr. Pauling and my orders stays orders till he gives me new ones. He's told me to let youse in here and to look after youse and that I'm doin', but never a word did he say about tellin' of youse anything, an' that I won't. What youse can see youse can see and welcome and what youse may overhear youse can hear, but I'd advise youse to not repeat it, and now draw your own conclusions.'"

The boys laughed. "He looked like that," said Frank. "I can just imagine him saying it."

"And what did you say?" inquired Mrs. Pauling. "I have met that man Murphy—he's one of Fred's right-hand men."

"Oh, I knew he was right and just slapped him on the back and told him he was a good skate and I'd put in a good word for him at any time. Told him I didn't want to butt in and wouldn't bother him with any more questions."

"Didn't you see anything?" asked Tom.

"About as much as you could see when we were in the crowd in the car," laughed Rawlins. "The garage wasn't packed full, but there were about a million plain-clothes men and police there and Lord knows how many trucks, and everything that was going on was in the center. But I did see them piling a lot of boxes and papers and a lot of radio stuff into a truck and I heard a policeman smack his lips and say: 'Glory be, but it's a burnin' shame to think of all the good booze that's goin' to waste nowadays. Sure it makes me throat feel dry as a load of hay to think of it.'"

"Perhaps," suggested Mrs. Pauling. "These men you found have some connection with the Bolshevist threats and crimes that the papers say are taking place. Fred never lets us know much of what is going on, as he thinks I'll worry. But whatever it is, I feel sure it has something to do with the troubles and worries Fred has had recently. Both he and Mr. Henderson have been working hard both day and night on something and Fred has looked as if he had some great problem on his mind."

"Well, I hope it's that," declared Tom. "Say, wouldn't it be great if we really *had* helped Dad and the government on something more important than smuggling liquor."

"There's the bell again," exclaimed Frank. "Perhaps that's Mr. Murphy."

Frank's surmise proved correct and Mrs. Pauling repeated her husband's orders to him. Scarcely waiting to hear, the detective turned and hurried off.

"I suppose we might as well have dinner," said Mrs. Pauling, after Murphy had gone. "There's no use waiting for Fred, he may be away all night. You'll have dinner with us, won't you, Mr. Rawlins?"

Dinner over, the four returned to the library and hour after hour dragged on with no word from Mr. Pauling.

Finally, Rawlins rose to go and was saying good night when the front door opened and Mr. Pauling, Mr. Henderson and the detective Murphy arrived.

"Didn't wait dinner for me, did you?" cried Tom's father, a note in his voice that his wife knew meant relief and elation. "Glad you didn't. Sorry we were so late, but couldn't get away a minute sooner. Didn't even have a chance to telephone to you. But we're as hungry as bears. I suppose there's a bite to eat."

Then, seeing Rawlins, hat in hand, he continued, "Don't go, Rawlins. Soon as we've eaten we'll try to satisfy your curiosity and the boys' and," he added mischievously, "the wife's, even if she does say she hasn't any."

"They're in mighty good spirits," declared Rawlins when the three men had disappeared in the direction of the dining room. "So I guess everything's come out O. K."

"Yes, Fred's had a great load lifted from his mind, I know," agreed Mrs. Pauling, "and I'm very glad. I've really been worried about him lately."

"Well, we'll soon know what 'tis," said Tom. "Gosh! I can scarcely wait."

At last they heard the voices of the three men, laughing and chatting, as they left the dining room, and an instant later they entered the library.

"Now I suppose you four want the truth, the whole truth and nothing but the truth," laughed Mr. Pauling, as he motioned the others to seats and settled himself in his own favorite chair. "I don't think there's much that I cannot reveal now—except a few matters which have no direct bearing or interest on the part you boys and Mr. Rawlins have played. Well, let's see. I guess I'd better begin at the garage—you know already that Henderson identified the prisoner and how we had a hunch that the affair centered in that block where the boys' radio compasses located the phantom speaker. I had an idea our men would have to surround the entire block and make a house-to-house search, but the rascals saved us that trouble. Evidently their friends had warned them that something was wrong and Reilly's men arrived just in time. They found a truck just leaving the garage, and, remembering my orders to hold every one and everything that looked suspicious, they stopped the truck—when the driver put on speed as soon as he glimpsed the police. That was suspicious and when they overhauled it they found it loaded with liquor. Inside the garage, they found four more trucks and a crowd of men and Murphy here tells me they put up a mighty good fight. That, of course, drew a crowd and East Side crowds have no use for the blue coats. The result was a free for all until another wagon arrived with reserves and in the fracas several of the men in the garage broke away and disappeared in the crowd.

"However, they got six and found enough contraband liquor in the trucks and in a secret room under the floor to stock a dozen saloons. Most of it was in this hidden room or cell under the floor, and very cleverly hidden, too. Had a door formed by a false bottom to a repair pit and all they had to do was to run a truck over the pit as if being repaired and pass up the goods from below. There were other things in that room, too. About twenty-five thousands dollars' worth of furs and jewelry—all stolen here or hereabouts; opium to the value of a hundred thousand or so, to say nothing of morphine, cocaine and other drugs. In addition, there were several thousand copies of red propaganda circulars and pamphlets, a neat little engraving and printing plant and a second trapdoor that opened into the old sewer. And the radio set was there also. A receiving set—made in Germany by the way—and the transmission outfit. That was the cleverest thing yet—according to Henderson who knows more about it than I do. He tells me the what-do-you-call-it—aërial—was a folding affair stretched across the inside of the roof and so arranged that it could be drawn back between the girders entirely out of sight. Now I don't know any of the technical part of this and I'll let Henderson explain it all to you boys later if you wish. But the main thing, as I understand it, was that they could send several thousand miles with the outfit on one kind of a wave or could talk to a person a few blocks away with another sort. At any rate, we never would have found that if we hadn't found the secret cell and the machine and a man at it. I'm not surprised Henderson's men never located it.

"That's all about the garage. It was the headquarters and clearing house of a dangerous gang of international cutthroats and rogues. They had been robbing right and left, carrying their loot in motor cars and trucks to the garage and hiding it in the secret room. Then from there it had been carried in watertight containers, like miniature submarines, through the old sewer to the submarine by the divers. Each time the submarine came in she brought a cargo of liquor, drugs, cigars, plumes, and other contraband and took away all the valuables and receipts from sales. The conversations you overheard were between those in the garage and other members of the gang, and the reason you boys did not hear the other speaker was because he used a radio telegraph instrument—that's right, isn't it, Henderson—and a very weak or short wave—let's see, a 'buzzer set' you called it, wasn't it? Well, you can get all that from Henderson, anyway."

"But how on earth did you find all that out?" asked Rawlins, as Mr. Pauling ceased speaking to light a cigar.

"Well, it took a little urging," replied Mr. Pauling. "Murphy and his men hinted to their prisoners that they'd been given the tip by the men on the submarine and so, of course, they told all they knew in the hope of getting lighter sentences and Henderson had the Russian up at his office with Ivan and let *him* think we knew all about him and the submarine through tips given by the other crowd. As a result, we got pretty complete information from both sides. But"—here Mr. Pauling lowered his voice and signaled for Murphy to stand guard at the door— "we couldn't get what we wanted from either the Russian or any of the gang at the garage. They'd tell us certain things—give us details and facts about matters of which we already knew— such as the means of communication, the submarine, etc., but beyond that they would not go.

"Short of torture I don't believe they'd let out a word. And we knew—we were positive—that back of it all was something deeper—a stupendous plot aimed at the very heart and life— the very existence of the United States and England. And we felt equally positive that back of this was an arch criminal or rather arch fiend—a man with a tremendous brain, almost unlimited power and marvelous resources. We could see many things which linked this petty smuggling, the hold-ups and burglaries, the rum-running and drug-importing with events of far greater importance. But we had no proof, no evidence to go on.

"Some of our men thought they knew who this head—this nucleus of the whole affair was but they could not be sure—they would not even dare mention his name—and so we were handicapped, working in the dark. But now we do know. We know far more than I dare tell any one, than I dare think. The injured man has placed it all in our hands. It was the most astounding revelation I have ever known or ever expect to hear. I cannot tell you all—I did not even permit Murphy or the doctor to be by the man's bedside while he spoke and as soon as I knew he could speak and understand English I sent Ivan off, too. Only Henderson and I heard what he said. This man was—yes, I say 'was,' because he is dead—was one of those misguided men who plotted against England and became a tool of the Germans. He betrayed his cause and his leaders, and, despised, hunted for the traitor and coward that he was, not safe either in England, Ireland or Germany, he became a man without a country, an enemy of all organized governments, a fanatical 'red' and a trusted emissary of this arch criminal I referred to.

"When he became conscious he raved and cursed frightfully, swearing he had been betrayed and in his mad desire for vengeance—knowing he had but a few moments to live—told us as best he could with his scorched and blackened lips and tongue what we longed to know. It was unbelievable, incredible, more marvelous than Jules Verne's stories, but true, we know, from the way it dovetails in with other facts in our possession.

"Among other things, we learned that many mysteriously missing ships—the many passenger and merchant vessels which never reached port—were deliberately sunk, torpedoed without warning and all survivors put to death in cold blood merely to secure the gold and other valuables on board. All this treasure, all the loot from robberies and crimes committed in the United States and abroad, all the receipts from smuggling and the sales of drugs and liquors were to swell the fund this master plotter was accumulating to accomplish his final purpose.

"This he told us towards the last—when each breath was a mighty effort, when each word was wrung from him with torture—and he even tried to tell us where it was hidden, where this vast treasure is concealed, cachéd, and where we might find the headquarters of this monster in human form. He was telling us and was striving, straining to give us the location. He had mentioned the locality in a general way, was giving us the latitude and longitude and had gasped out three figures when he died—the words unfinished, the secret sealed within his lips and—most important of all, with the name of that ruthless, relentless master-fiend unspoken."

The boys' eyes had grown round with wonder as Mr. Pauling was speaking. Mrs. Pauling leaned forward, her face flushed, her lips parted. Rawlins had remained as silent, as immovable as if carved in stone, and even Mr. Henderson and Murphy had been so engrossed, so interested, although they knew the story as well as Mr. Pauling, that they had allowed their cigars to go out.

"Jehoshaphat!" exclaimed Tom, when his father ceased speaking. "Gosh! We *did* butt into something worth while!"

"Oh, Gee!" ejaculated Frank in disappointed tones. "Then you don't know where that treasure is after all!"

"No," replied Mr. Pauling, "not within several hundred miles. But the treasure is not the important thing, it's the man himself we want."

Rawlins rose, his eyes shone with unwonted brilliancy, his face was flushed.

"I'll say that's some day's work!" he cried. "But I'll bet we *can* get that loot—and that whole bunch of crooks, too. I've a scheme, Mr. Pauling, but I want a little time to think it over and get my brain straightened out. There's been too much crowded into it during the last ten hours."

Mr. Pauling stared at Rawlins as if he thought he might have taken leave of his senses. Then, realizing that Rawlins was in earnest, he said quietly, "All right, Rawlins. I don't know what your scheme may be, but I'll be glad to hear it whenever you're ready. Call me up and we'll hear it when you have it worked out. We owe you more than I can express to you now."

A moment later Rawlins had gone and hardly had his footsteps died away when the telephone tinkled.

"Yes!" exclaimed Mr. Pauling as he listened. "Remarkable! Absolutely deserted! Well, I guess that chapter's closed. Thanks for letting me know."

"Sorry Rawlins has gone," declared Mr. Pauling as he hung up the receiver and wheeled about. "That was the Admiral calling. One of the destroyers has found the submarine!"

"Gosh! then they've caught more of the gang!" cried Tom.

"That's the astounding part of it," replied his father. "She was found drifting, her upper works just awash, about one hundred miles out to sea and *not a living soul on board her*!"

CHAPTER XIII—RAWLINS' PROPOSAL

When Rawlins called on Mr. Pauling the following day the first thing that greeted him was the announcement that the submarine had been found.

So excited were the boys that for some time they could not convey an intelligible idea of the matter and before Rawlins could grasp the details of the discovery they were plying him with questions as to his opinion in regard to it.

"What do you think became of the men?" cried Tom.

"Do you suppose it was their boat?" demanded Frank.

"How do you think it got so far away, if it's theirs?" put in Tom.

"We puzzled over it for hours last night and no one can explain it," declared Frank.

"Easy, boys, easy!" laughed Rawlins. "One thing at a time. Shorten sails a bit and let me get my bearings. You say the destroyer found a submarine floating just awash and absolutely deserted one hundred miles off the coast? I don't believe it *was* that sub!"

"Could you identify it by a description—anything about it?" asked Mr. Pauling.

"Well, I don't know," admitted Rawlins. "I know it was a German sub and I'd recognize it if I saw it; but whether I can be sure of it by a description depends upon the description."

"They're towing her in," Mr. Pauling informed him. "She was disabled and unable to come in under her own power. Until she arrives all we know is that she is a German boat—one of the medium-sized craft—that she carries torpedoes and a gun and that she is painted sea-green."

"Fits her like an Easter bonnet," declared Rawlins. "Under water I could not be sure of her color, but it was not black or gray—everything takes on a greenish look under water. Did they find anything suspicious on her?"

"That I can't say," replied Mr. Pauling. "They didn't report whether they made any discoveries or not."

"But if it *is* the submarine, where are the men?" reiterated Tom.

"Search me," replied Rawlins. "A lot of things may have happened to them. Something may have gone wrong so they were obliged to come up and knowing they would be captured they took the sub's boats. Or again, they may have decided to desert the sub and scatter—probably they knew the chaps we got, and suspected they'd confess. It would have been an easy matter to run in close to shore, take to the boats and land and then sink the boats in shallow water so as to leave no trace. Or some ship might have picked them up. By the way, I've been puzzling over something. How do you suppose that sub got in and out of the West Indies without being seen and reported. If she carried contraband in and loot out she must have gone to some port."

"Why, didn't I explain that?" asked Mr. Pauling. "Must have slipped my mind when relating the story yesterday. The prisoner told us how they managed. The submarine never entered any port—unless you consider the hiding place of the chief of the gang a port—but picked up her cargoes in mid-ocean."

"Oh, I see, transferred them from another ship, eh?" said Rawlins. "Stupid of me not to think of it."

"Not quite right yet, Rawlins," chuckled Mr. Pauling. "It was this way. A vessel would sail from a West Indian port with a cargo and would drop it overboard at a designated spot. Then the submarine would pick it up. If they had transferred on the surface they might have been seen and rough weather would have interfered. Moreover, if those on the schooners saw the submarine or knew of her they might have talked. They imagined the things were to be grappled or brought up by divers. The head of this bunch takes no chances."

"Ah, now I see a light dawning!" exclaimed Rawlins. "I think that solves several puzzles. You remember those messages you boys heard? Well, they always, or nearly always, included numbers—'thirty-eight fifty, seventy-seven' was one, I believe—and 'good bottom' and similar things. I often wondered about those, but I'll bet those were the spots where the sub was to find cargoes dumped. Hasn't that Russian Johnny come across with anything more about the high Muck-a-Muck of the bunch and where he hangs out?"

"No, I had another long session with him, but he swears he knows nothing about it and for once I am inclined to think he is telling the truth," replied Mr. Pauling. "He insists that he never visited the place—never saw the chief and does not even know who he is—except that all spoke of him as of a supreme being or a king. His story is that only a few men—just enough to man the submarine—including the fellow who died, went to headquarters. That the others, including himself, were always put ashore at a small island in the West Indies where they had a camp and that they walked to the island from the submarine and from the shore to their under-sea craft in diving suits."

"That's a probable yarn," assented Rawlins. "Did he tell you the name of the island?"

"He says he doesn't know it himself, that there were a few natives there when he first arrived, but that under orders from their superiors they murdered the blacks in cold blood."

"Dirty swine, I'll say!" exclaimed Rawlins. "Well, I know the West Indies a lot better than I know New York and if we can squeeze some sort of a description from old pig-eye I'll wager

I can locate that hangout. But now about that other business—those messages—have you got the notes you made of them, boys?"

"Sure," replied Tom, "At least, Mr. Henderson has. We gave them all to him."

"Well, we'll need 'em if Mr. Pauling thinks my proposition all right," said Rawlins. "I hadn't got it quite settled as to details when I came in, but the capture of that sub—if she is the one—has cleared it all up."

"I can tell you better what I think of any proposal you may have after I have heard it," said Mr. Pauling.

"All right, here goes," laughed Rawlins. "You see from what you told us about that dead fellow's confession, I am pretty sure the big 'I am' of the bunch is hanging out somewhere in the West Indies. You said he was giving you the place and had mentioned three figures of latitude and longitude when he kicked off. Now I don't know what those figures are, but there are not such an everlasting lot of combinations of figures in the islands—that is, where a man could have a secret hangout—and I know 'em like a book—better than any book in fact—and if I had those figures I'll bet I can locate the old Buckaroo. Not only that, but with my suits and the boys' radio and my submarine chamber—the same as I use for taking under-sea pictures—we could get the loot and everything else if he's got any of it under water.

"I rather figured, from what you said, that might be where he'd hide it, especially as he seems stuck on under-sea work. Why, if the old cove himself had a house under the sea I could find him! If they used this new-fangled radio under water up here you can bet your boots the old guy's using it where he hangs out and if we're any place near we can pick him up and the boys can locate him with that radio compass business. You see he probably won't be wise to any one else being on to the radio business. I was afraid that sub might get back and give it away, but the chances are that if the men aboard her got ashore they either won't dare show up down there and will just fade away or else we can beat 'em to it.

"Taking that sub gave me another idea and a good one. We can fix up the old boat and go scouting for old Stick-in-the-mud in that. If he or any of his gang see her they'll think it's all right and that their gang's still in her. I know a pretty good lot about handling a sub and we can pick up a few good ex-navy men I know. Now don't you think that's a corking good scheme, Mr. Pauling?"

Mr. Pauling hestitated, thinking deeply, before he spoke.

"It has its good points," he admitted at last, "but it's rather a wild scheme—just what I should expect from a boy who'll tackle two strangers and a submarine single-handed under water—and there's not one chance in ten thousand that it will succeed. You see, the West Indies are a pretty good-sized place and you'd have to go by guess work a great deal, even with the figures the man gave us. However, I'm willing to aid and abet the scheme, as any chance—no matter how remote—of getting that arch fiend is worth trying. I can get the submarine without trouble and can secure men who can be depended upon, but who's going with you on your wild-goose or wild-man chase?"

"Why, we are!" cried Tom and Frank in unison.

"The dickens you are!" exclaimed Mr. Pauling. "I should say not!"

The boys' faces fell. "Oh, Dad, please let us go," begged Tom. "It will be great—going in a submarine and trying to find that fellow with our radio. Why won't you let us go?"

"Too much risk," replied his father. "I've had one fright over you and that's enough."

"Well, that rather knocks out my plans, too," declared Rawlins. "I'd counted on the boys going to work the radio end of it—seems kind of hard on them to let some one else do it after they invented the thing and were responsible for getting the men and the sub. If it hadn't been for them I'd never have got 'em, as it was their hearing Tom yell for help that made 'em surrender, and you'd never have thought of that block and the garage if they hadn't located those messages with their radio compasses. I don't think there's any danger, Mr. Pauling."

"I don't agree with you," declared Mr. Pauling in positive tones. "If you go after that man there's every danger. You can't tell what force he may use or how an attempt to capture him might turn out."

"But I had no idea of attempting to get him alone," replied Rawlins in surprise. "My plan was to have a trim little destroyer right handy and then, when we'd located Mr. Big Bug, we'd report to the jackies and let them do the dirty work. The boys wouldn't have to be where there was any scrapping going on and that old ex-German sub is never going to be my coffin if I can help it, I'll tell the world. No, sir, my idea was just to do the scouting, so to speak—secret service under the sea—and let the boys be in on the preliminary intelligence work running the secret service of the air as you might say."

"Well, I suppose in that case there would be little risk," admitted Mr. Pauling, "and as you say, they *are* really the ones who should be allowed to have charge of their own apparatus as they have earned the right to it. I'll have to give a little more consideration to the matter before I decide, however. Possibly I may wish to go along also—or I may be asked to, when I put this matter before my superiors. Now here are those figures given by the dying man and the notes made by the boys."

Unlocking a drawer, Mr. Pauling took out a packet of papers and spread them before Rawlins, while the two boys, now that events had taken a more hopeful and promising turn, laughed and talked excitedly to each other, wildly enthusiastic at the bare possibility of going on the unique search.

For a few minutes Rawlins studied the various sheets intently and silently, comparing the figures which the boys had heard spoken and the ones given by the dying Irishman, and at last he glanced up.

"These numbers of the boys' will need a lot of study," he declared, "but these the chap in the hospital gave are dead easy. One of 'em is nineteen and as there's no longitude nineteen in the West Indies, or within two thousand miles of the islands, it must be latitude, so there we have a clue right out of the box— nineteen north latitude. Now if we take a map and follow along nineteen we'll know it must be within a few miles of it that we'll locate old Beelzebub. It can't be over sixty miles north of that meridian or the man would have said twenty instead of nineteen, and it can't be south of it or he'd have said eighteen and something. So we can be dead sure the old duck hits the hay somewhere in a sixty-mile belt bounded by meridians nineteen and twenty. Now here are the other two numbers—sixty and seventy-five. You say he sort of lost consciousness between these and you thought he said southwest by south. Well, sixty might be longitude—the sixtieth meridian is in the West Indies—but he might have meant sixty anything and so, if it *is* longitude he was getting at, it brings us down to a space six hundred miles east and west and sixty miles north and south—quite a consid- erable bit of land and water to search—about 36,000 square miles—but only a little of it's land, so it don't cut such a figure. That'll take in—let's see—some of the Virgins, I think, and a lot of little cays and quite a bit of Santo Domingo, but shucks, that's not such a heap. But I'll admit this seventy-five gets my nanny. It's not minutes—'cause there are only sixty minutes to a degree and it's a dead sure cinch that it's not latitude or longi- tude if those other numbers are, and if it's latitude it would be in the Arctic instead of the Caribbean and if it's longitude it'll knock calculations out for about a thousand miles and will take in all of Santo Domingo and Haiti, a bit of Cuba and most of the Bahamas. Looks as if we might have some jaunt. And I don't get those compass bearings. However, maybe when they get that sub in and search her we'll find some chart or something. When do you expect—"

At this moment the telephone rang and Mr. Pauling answered.

"Ah, fine!" he exclaimed. "Expect to be in within an hour! Yes, I'd be glad to. I'm bringing some others with me—Mr. Rawlins and the boys. Yes, queer we were just talking of it. Good."

"It was the navy yard," explained Mr. Pauling as he hung up the receiver. "They say the submarine is coming in now and will be at the yard in half an hour. The Admiral wants me to be on hand to board her as soon as she arrives and I'd like you and the boys to come along."

"Hurrah!" yelled the two boys. "Now we'll see what they had on her."

"And we'll know if she's the right sub," added Rawlins. "Though it's dollars to doughnuts that she is—it's not likely there's more than one lost, strayed or stolen sub knocking about in these waters."

When they reached the Navy Yard the submarine was just being docked and twenty minutes later they were entering her open hatch. The boys had never been within a submarine before and were intensely interested in the machinery, the submerging devices, the air-locks and the torpedo tubes, but their greatest interest was in the radio room. But here, much to their chagrin and disappointment, they found practically nothing. There were a few wires, some discarded old-fashioned coils, some microphones and receivers and a loop aërial. Everything else had been removed and nothing was left to show what sort of instruments had been used. The boys were about to leave when Tom noticed something half-hidden under a coil of wire, and, curious to see what it might be, pulled it out.

"Gosh!" he exclaimed as he saw what it was. "These chaps were using that same single control. This is part of it. Look, Frank, the dial is just the same as the one Mr. Henderson gave us."

"Gee, that's right!" agreed Frank. "But then," he added, "after all it's not surprising. You know Mr. Henderson said the one he gave us came from a German U-boat."

"Not a thing in the radio room," announced Tom, as the boys rejoined Mr. Pauling. "Everything's stripped clean, but they used the same sort of tuner that Mr. Henderson gave us. Where's Mr. Rawlins?"

"Somewhere under our feet," laughed his father. "He went down to examine the hull. Wants to be sure this is the same boat."

A few moments later the door to the air-lock was opened and Rawlins appeared.

"I'll say it's the same old sub!" he exclaimed. "There's a dent in her skin near the stern on the port side. I noticed it before and it's there all right. Found anything up here?"

"No, nothing of any value to us," replied Mr. Pauling. "The boys say the radio's been stripped from her and we haven't been able to find a chart or a map or a scrap of paper aboard. We found two of those carriers though—the cigar-shaped affairs you saw the divers towing through the water; but they're both empty. If these fellows took anything from the garage they disposed of it before they left the submarine."

"Were the boats on her when they found her?" asked Rawlins.

"No, no sign of them," replied the officer who was with them. "I boarded her first thing, but there was no sign of life aboard and no boats."

"It's darned funny!" commented Rawlins. "If these lads took to the boats they did it deliberately and took mighty good care to clean the old sub out before they left. That disposes of the theory that they were compelled to leave. Do you know what the trouble was with her machinery, Commander?"

"Haven't found out yet," replied the officer. "We'll have the engineers aboard as soon as Mr. Pauling is through inspection."

"Didn't see any signs of small boats near where you found

her, did you?" inquired Rawlins.

The officer shook his head.

"No," he replied, "but it was pretty dark and they might have been within a few miles—very low visibility."

"And no other vessel that might have picked them up?" continued Rawlins.

"Not a sail in sight—except a fishing smack about ten miles off. We ran down to her and boarded her. Thought they might have sighted the sub, or picked up the men. They hadn't done either. Bunch of square-heads that didn't seem to know what a sub was, just dirty fishermen."

"Dead sure they were?" asked Rawlins. "Didn't notice where she hailed from, did you?"

The officer flushed.

"Afraid we didn't," he admitted, a trace of resentment at being questioned in his tones. "She hoisted sail soon after we left her."

"And nothing peculiar about her in any way, I suppose?" suggested Mr. Pauling.

"Well, I didn't see anything," replied the commander, "but I believe one of my bluejackets made some remark about her rig. He's a bo'sun's mate and an old man-o-warsman—Britisher but naturalized citizen and served in the British navy. Would you like to question him? I'm no expert on sailing craft myself."

"Better talk to him, Rawlins," suggested Mr. Pauling.

As there seemed nothing more to be discovered on the submarine the party left the under-sea craft and walked to the destroyer which had found her. The sailor to whom the officer had referred proved to be a grizzled old salt—a typical deep-sea sailor and the boys could not take their eyes from him. Touching his gray forelock in salute, the man hitched his trousers, squinted one eye and reflectively scratched his head just over his left ear.

"Yes, Sir," he said, in reply to Mr. Rawlins' question. "She *was* a bit queer, Sir. Blow me ef she warn't. Man an' boy Hi've been a sailorin' most thirty year an' strike me if Hi ever seed a Yankee smack the like o' her, Sir. What was it was queer about her, you're askin' on me? Well, Sir, 'twas like this, Sir. She had a bit too much rake to her marsts, Sir, an' a bit too high a dead-rise an' her starn warn't right an' her cutwater was diff'rent an' her cuddy. She carried a couple o' little kennels to port and sta'board o' her companion-way, Sir—same as those bloomin' West Hindian packets, Sir. An' as you know, Sir, most Yankee smacks carry main torpmas's and no fore-torpmas' while this e'er hooker was sportin' o' sticks slim an' lofty as a yacht's, Sir, an' a jib-boom what was a sprung a bit down, Sir. But what got my bally goat, Sir, was the crew. Mos' of 'em was Scandinav'ans, Sir, but the skipper was a mulatter or somethin' o' that specie, Sir, an' blow me hif he didn't talk with a haccent what might ha' been learnt at Wapping, Sir."

Rawlins whistled.

"I'll say there was something queer about her!" he exclaimed. "Anything else? Did you note her name and port?"

Once more the old sailor scratched his head and shifted the tobacco in his cheek before replying.

"Cawn't say as how Hi did, Sir," he announced at last. "You see, Sir, she had her mainsail lowered, Sir, and a hangin' a bit sloppy over her stern, Sir, an' we was alongside an' didn't pass under her stern, Sir."

"What sort of boats did she carry and how many?" asked Rawlins.

"Dories, Sir, six of 'em," replied the sailor, "anything more, Sir?"

"No, I think that's all. Thanks for the information," replied Rawlins and then, reaching in his pocket he handed the man several cigars.

Touching his forelock again and with a final hitch of his trousers the sailor turned and strolled off with the rolling gait of the true deep-water seaman.

"Well, what do you make of it?" asked Mr. Pauling, when the sailor was out of earshot.

"I'll say it's blamed funny that packet was hanging around near the sub," replied Rawlins. "It might be a coincidence—Bahama smacks *do* come pretty well up here during the summer—and she might have been a rum-runner, but putting two and two together I'd say she was waiting for the sub and that the crew were on board her when the destroyer came up."

"Jove!" ejaculated Mr. Pauling. "Then you think she was a West Indian boat?"

"I don't think, I know!" answered Rawlins. "A Bahama schooner—not any doubt of that. Only Caribbean craft carry those two deck-houses and that sprung jib-boom and the darkey skipper with the English accent just clinches it. I'll bet those square-heads were Russian Johnnies or Huns off this darn sub. Say, if we don't get a move on they'll beat us to the islands yet!"

"Gosh!" exclaimed Tom. "I'll bet they took their radio outfit aboard."

"I'll say they did!" declared Rawlins. "And like as not they'll be under full sail for the Caribbean by now and working that radio overtime to get word to the old High Panjandrum down there."

"Not if I know it!" cried Mr. Pauling. "Come along, Rawlins. I'm going to see the Admiral."

The result of that hurried and exceedingly confidential interview was that, as the boys and Mr. Rawlins were crossing the Manhattan Bridge in Mr. Pauling's car, they looked down and saw a lean, gray destroyer sweeping down the river with two others in her wake, black smoke pouring from their funnels, great mounds of foam about their bows and screeching an almost incessant warning from their sirens as they sped seawards bearing orders to overhaul and capture a Bahama schooner that, under a cloud of canvas, was plunging southward on the farther edge of the Gulf Stream, her mulatto skipper driving his craft to her utmost, while aloft two monkeylike negro seamen were busily stretching a pair of slender wires between the straining lofty topmasts.

Two days later, a black-hulled liner steamed out from New York's harbor and dropping her pilot also headed southward for the Bahamas. Upon her decks stood Tom and Frank with Mr. Pauling and Mr. Henderson by their sides, while in the Navy Yard, with a marine guard tramping ceaselessly back and forth about her, a submarine was being feverishly fitted for a long cruise.

After much discussion, Mr. Pauling had at last given consent to the boys joining in the search for the mysterious master mind whose plans had so far come to grief through their efforts, although he refused to consider letting them go south on the captured submarine. But the boys had no objections to this, for they did not look forward with any pleasure to an ocean voyage in the sub-sea boat and were filled with excitement at the thoughts of the adventures in store for them when they joined Rawlins, and the submarine at a prearranged meeting place in the Bahamas.

As they watched the skyline of New York fade into the mists of the summer afternoon and the smooth gray-green sea stretched before them beyond the Narrows, they were thinking of the adventures which had so strangely fallen to their lot in the great city and Tom chuckled.

"Remember when we first called ourselves radio detectives?" he asked Frank, "Gosh! We never thought we'd even strike anything the way we did."

"You bet I do!" rejoined Frank. "Say, wasn't Henry sore because he couldn't go and wasn't he crazy to find out what we were going for? It's great! And we're real radio detectives now—working for Uncle Sam, too!"

"Rather, I should say, 'radio secret service,'" said Mr. Henderson who stood beside them. "But don't talk about it.

Remember the first thing for a person in this service to learn is to hear everything, see everything, Paul and say nothing."

"We will!" declared the boys in unison.

"That'll be our motto!" added Tom. "Isn't it a bully one?"

"As Mr. Rawlins would say, 'I'll say it is'!" said Frank.

THE END

www.ingramcontent.com/pod-product-compliance
Lightning Source LLC
Chambersburg PA
CBHW020915180626

46816CB00007BA/2410